THE SPIRIT OF
CHRISTMAS 1940

CONTENTS

Foreword

The Spirit of Christmas 1940 has actually been played out in my mind so many times in varying formats. Believe it or not, it actually started out life as a musical. Many songs were written to carry the story through but the more and more I wrote, the more the story became a Christmas tale that needed to be written as a book.

I cannot begin to tell you the amount of influences that have driven me to write this book. From a long and difficult military career, to a deep interest of war-time Britain. There is even a hint of Mr Dickens there, not that I would ever compare myself to the great man.

Setting the story at the time of the Blitz gave me a unique opportunity to develop a hidden story of everyday folk in one of the most testing times our country has ever seen. I hope it pays homage to those brave, resilient soles who refused to let a bully dictate their way of life.

Of course, there is a strong fictitious element as you will soon see but I have endeavored to keep the story accurate for the time period. However, I apologise in advance for any unintentional inaccuracies. But please do bear in mind it is just a story.

Finally, I would like to thank my wonderful partner for her support and encouragement while I wrote our story. Every man needs a rock on which to build his church, Jane has proved time and time again to be the foundation for my life's Cathedral and I would like to dedicate this book to her devotion.

For Jane
&
Great Uncle William

ACKNOWLEDGEMENTS

THE SOLDIER & THE STATION

I feel it is important, before jumping into the book, to explain two major factors of the story and the real influences behind them.

Firstly, and to me most importantly, the soldier, Rifleman William Snow. He was a very real soldier who served in WW1 as described later in this book and as stated, he was killed on the date and during the battle also mentioned. How do I know all of this? Because he was my grandmothers uncle, Unfortunately very few relatives of William remain today so I felt it would be fitting to pay tribute to him by immortalising his name within this book, albeit in a fictitious story.

But to me, William Snow has been more than a mere influence for a book character. I first came upon him some years ago after my sister carried out a search of our family tree. She mentioned to me that she had found somebody who had served in the army during the Great War and wondered if I could use my military connections to research him. Well, I found the lot. The big clue being the cemetery where he was buried. William lies in La Neuville British War Cemetery, Corbie, France. This was just one of the many graveyards used for those who fell during the Somme campaign.

William was born in Smethwick, Staffs in 1894 and joined 11th Bn Rifle Brigade. He was just 22 at the time of his death while carrying out a counter-offensive at the Battle of Delville Wood. He was mortally wounded on 31st August 1916, finally dying of his wounds the following day.

So, learning that I had a great, great uncle has filled me with tremendous pride but I can't help feeling he has been somewhat forgotten. Of course, he is just one soldier out of thousands upon thousands that remain in France but he is a distant relative and hopefully, this book will keep his memory alive.

Secondly, is the station the story is set in. Although I had a typical Victorian style London train station in mind, it was hard to picture the scenes unfolding without being able to take in an actual station. That was until we visited the Great Western Railway Station in Kidderminster. OK, it wasn't in London but it was beautifully set and almost exactly as I imagined it.

We have spent many hours at the GWR station just taking in the inspiration which has made writing this story so much easier. I must also say a huge thanks to the staff at the station who have inspired many of the characters in this book. I wondered if the same spirit that existed at Kidderminster was a true reflection of what life was really like back during the war. Just a few hundred yards from GWR Kidderminster is the towns main station with the usual humdrum of the rat race of the noughties. It's cold, unfriendly and very impersonal. But just a few feet away you step into a world where you find hope and happiness. I have to suggest a trip there for you all. It's truly a wonderful day out'

Between William Snow and GWR Kidderminster, the story just about tells itself. These are the foundations of The Spirit of Christmas 1940. Everything else you read of course is fiction but do bear in mind the reality that exists within the story. Before we embark on our journey, I'd like to finish this acknowledgment with the inscription on great uncle Williams grave stone. I feel it's kind of fitting for our story.

'TO LIVE IN HEARTS WE LEAVE BEHIND IS NOT TO DIE'

CHAPTER ONE

CHURCH STREET

The cold, grey figure of a soldier stood at the entrance to Platform one. He was dressed in the uniform of the Rifle Brigade from the Great War and, although Church Street station was used frequently by servicemen travelling to and from various military stations around the UK, he stood out like a sore thumb. His stare was empty as if he was void of conciousness but nothing could be further from the truth as he battled with the fear and disbelief of how he came to be standing on this platform.

Pre-Christmas preparations at Church Street Station in the heartland of London were proving to be something of a nightmare as 1940 was coming to a close. London had been at the mercy of the Luftwaffe since September and the constant bombardments were taking its toll on the tired old station, although, thankfully, it was yet to take a direct hit. Still, the scars from nearby flying debris remained apparent on the face of the outside walls and windows.

The station platform was still, apart from a few trade stalls being prepared for the onslaught of daily commuters and a tired old man lazily pushed a broom around the station mumbling quietly to himself. The first of the outgoing passengers began wandering in looking bleary eyed in the early morning cold air.

Church Street Station was a beautiful old station built in the heart of London in the late 1800's. The Victorian style architecture was typical of many of the major city stations such as Kings Cross and Waterloo although somewhat smaller. Still, the station was large enough to house many businesses within the buildings such as shops, a cafe and even it's own pub. It really was a small village within four walls. Inside the station was a large main area where trade stands conducted their business, passengers would meet and greet and information boards would show the daily schedules from four platforms that would receive the locomotives and passenger cars from every corner of Great Britain. In addition to it's main rail platforms, Church street was also part of the underground tube network. Although during these troubled times, the undergrounds main role was very quickly turning into air raid shelters. Church Street was no different.

A suited man emerged from the station office, carrying a bag stuffed full of crude Christmas decorations ready to adorn the tree that sat beneath the station clock. Despite the constant air raid warnings and piles of rubble lining the streets around the station, Mr Crispin was determined to ensure that his patrons could, at least, be reminded of the spirit of Christmas. James Crispin was a clean cut, efficient man who ruled his station kingdom with authority and precision. He was a proud man who, although approaching his sixties, had the bearing of former military man. In fact, he was a veteran of the trenches of the Great War. He never spoke much about it, he didn't want to have folks feel sorry for him or tell him how much of a hero he was. That was not Mr Crispin at all. But for now, he was the station Christmas tree decorator. At least it would give him an hour or two not thinking about the relentless bombing runs from those damn planes.

Apart from the Christmas tree, there were very few other decorations reminding people of the forthcoming celebrations. Maybe the only other reminders were the Holly wreaths on Rose's flower cart. Mr Crispin had a little soft spot for the young Rose. She was always so cheerful and friendly. She always made him feel that happiness could always be found at Church Street.

His thoughts were interrupted by the sharp whistling of the arrival of the 5:30am postal train. Ah well, the decorations would have to wait. He walked over to the platform to meet the guard as

Chapter 1

he stepped off the train.

The quietness and peace of the station was disturbed not only by the mail train but also the arrival of Jimmy Deacon, the station newspaper vendor. A cheeky east-end lad cursed with an over active sense of humour, and far too much confidence for his own good. He had been selling the Daily Herald in exactly the same spot since leaving school. Not much of a career but he could always make up for his low wages by a few 'under the table' deals from his many east end contacts. Everybody knew that his goods originated 'off the back of a lorry' but nobody questioned it. Even the local police turned a blind eye as they knew he wouldn't overcharge people and he could often be a blessing at this time of strict rationing. In fact, a visit by the police to the station was normally just an excuse for them to grab a bargain from Jimmy when nobody was watching. Besides there was never any point in questioning Jimmy about the origin of his stock as he had the gift of the gab and could talk his way out of anything so to save time, energy and an awful lot of wasted paperwork, they just turned a blind eye as long as he didn't go too far.

Within ten minutes, his newspaper stand was set up and his daily act began. "Read all abaht it, Joe Louis wins heavyweight title. Get yer 'erald 'ere" The headlines would be screamed out over and over the next few hours enticing passengers to part with a penny for the latest edition. Just as Jimmy was about to yell out once again, he was stopped dead in his tracks, his mouth left open as if his jaw had suddenly frozen. The reason for the shock was the entrance of the flower barrow being pushed onto the platform by Rose.

Rose provided such a vital service to the many customers of Church Street station providing flowers for the reuniting husbands and wives, girlfriends and boyfriends, mothers, daughters fathers, sons and of course, for the servicemen and women returning from the war. Christmas, though, was a good opportunity to lift spirits with holly wreaths, mistletoe and all sorts of decorations for family Christmas trees, mantelpieces and dinner tables. But although the station needed her, she also needed the station, and her stall. Rose was an only child and the only source of income for her dad who had lost his legs during the First World War. Her mother had died when she was just a young girl leaving Rose to grow up faster than she wanted. Still, she made ends meet and for the most of the time, she and her dad were ok.

Her flower stall was an old wooden cart but beautifully set up with all sorts of flowers and plants which brought the tired wood to life. The colours were simply stunning and to add to the magic, were the seasonal special extras. Just perfect. But despite the beauty there was still a job to do.

As Rose prepared for the days business, she was still being stared at by the unwitting Jimmy. He had been besotted by Rose ever since he had been selling papers at the station. But although he had a very over-confident attitude, it was just a front. Underneath the Cockney charm, Jimmy was a bit of an introvert when it came to talking to the opposite sex. Rosie, as he called her, was the one he feared the most. Certainly not because there was anything scary about her but because he had so many feelings for her. He could never bring himself to go over and tell her, instead he would ply her with gifts from his dodgy dealings. He thought to himself that if he could look after her then maybe one day it would just happen. She may see how he felt and make the first move. Or at least, that was the theory. The problem was, Rose was just as shy. Of course she felt the same for Jimmy but her innocence and natural shyness prevented her from ever telling him. To everybody that knew them, including a great many of the regular passengers to Church Street, It was blatantly obvious that these two were an item.

As both, Rose and Jimmy prepared for the day ahead, the station was slowly filling up with people looking to start their daily journey's or arriving to meet passengers coming in from all over the country. The station cafe and stalls were opening up for the day and the staff who controlled the daily mayhem were rolling up ready to greet another day at Church Street Station.

Today was also another day for the mysterious soldier who still remained at the entrance to Platform one waiting to discover the reason why he had found himself in this new, strange world.

CHAPTER TWO

THE SOLDIER

For over a year, Great Britain had been in the grip of the second major war of the twentieth century. Hitler's war machine had been marching across Europe with a devastating ferocity until it came to the small island called Great Britain. Earlier during 1940, the Luftwaffe had attempted to dominate the air in what was to be known as the Battle of Britain. However, Hitler didn't count on the sheer determination of the Royal Air Force and by July, the German offensive on Britain had failed.

However, for the next eight months, the air attacks on the airfields turned to bombing runs over the capital and other major cities such as Hull, Liverpool, Southampton, Portsmouth and other strategic targets. So began the Blitz. London was to lose around 20,000 civilians during the raids before the Blitz ended. Despite the horrific loss of life and mass damage to the cities, Hitler failed in his plan to disrupt the manufacture of munitions and equipment.

As for Church Street, the old station had remained mostly intact except for some minor shrapnel damage on the outside walls. However the daily comings and going of servicemen inside told a much different story. Every day, troops were gathering on mass on the platforms to head to the ports on their way to the many battlefields. And everyday, troops were arriving on the platform after being shipped back home from playing their part. Some limbless, some blind, most shell-shocked. Families would arrive to meet their loved ones, some waited in vain.

In some cases, officers would wait on the platform to inform relatives of the loss of their brave family members, It was a truly heartbreaking sight. Jimmy would always be on the look out for such instances, the last thing he wanted to do would be to scream out the latest headlines when such devastating scenes were happening. The quick minded Jimmy always knew when to keep quiet. Happily, this was not one of those times but something had caught his interest. He wandered across the platform to Rose who was busy arranging her displays of flowers into stunning colourful patterns.

"Ere Rosie, have you seen that soldier over there? He looks different to all the rest of 'em".

Rose peered across to a tall solitary soldier standing by the ticket booth by Platform 1. His face was completely expressionless and seemed oblivious to the hustle and bustle of the station. Almost as if he occupied a space completely separated from normal daily life.

"I can't say I noticed him" Rosie replied, although she had indeed seen him earlier as she arrived. Something about him had caught her eye, something eerie but safe. Something that couldn't quite be explained. But she dismissed her thoughts. Best leave him be, besides he appeared so sad as if he knew the pain that was bound to be arriving at church street before long.

Jimmy scratched his head in wonder. "I wonder who he is? He don't seem right to me."

"Best just let him alone Jimmy. It's not our business." Rosie didn't want to labour the subject. She felt uncomfortable getting involved in other people's business.

"I'm surprised old Crispin hasn't told him to sling his hook. You know what he gets like when things don't seem right. Still, I suppose you're right." Jimmy thought it might be a good idea to change the subject. "Anyway, when you gonna come dancin' with me? I keep askin' but your always too busy. I get the feeling you're giving me the brush." He said cheekily.

Rose giggled. "You know I'd love to come out with you but you know how busy I am especially with dad the way he is. We'll see. Maybe after Christmas , eh?

"Oh alright, I'll wait, but you got to have a bit of time for yourself. All you ever do is work here or look after your old man. You got a big heart Rosie, but you'll burn yourself out if you ain't careful."

Rose knew Jimmy was right. She loved her dad and would do absolutely anything to make sure he was ok but being his only carer and the only source of income in these desperate times meant that she missed out on the life other young ladies had. Friends, fun and love were just dreams out of reach. But she was grateful for Jimmy. He was like a guardian angel. Of course, there was no doubt he loved her but she knew he would never see her go without. Still, it wasn't fair to return any kind of affection at the moment. They would only both get hurt. Maybe things would change once this mad war had ended.

Jimmy looked around suspiciously, as if he was a spy about to pass on a big secret to another agent. He slipped his hand into the inside of his coat and sneakily pulled out a newspaper wrapped parcel.

"Ere, stick this under your cart. Somethin' nice for you and your dads tea.

"What is it?" Rose asked.

"A full pound of best bacon. Got it special this morning. Don't tell anyone though, if word gets out, Brian the Butcher will kick my arse from here to kingdom come."

"Jimmy, you're not going to get in to trouble for this, are you? I don't want to be part of anything that lands you in hot water."

"Nah, don't worry. As long as the coppers still buy from me I'm ok. I just don't want that old skinflint getting wind of where I get my little deals from. He would just charge people over the odds just so he could line his own pocket. It's not so much that I'm scared of getting caught, I just don't want that old bugger ripping people off."

Rose smiled and slipped the package on the shelf below her cart. She picked up a small red rose and put it into the button hole of Jimmy's coat and gave him a little kiss on the cheek. "Thank you."

Jimmy turned a deep red as he blushed uncontrollably. It was if all of his emotions had just been whisked up in the mixing bowl of his head and he was suddenly and completely at Rose's mercy.

His embarrassment was suddenly interrupted by the shriek of another arriving train. As normal, Jimmy looked across to make sure he wasn't going to shout out at an awkward moment. His eyes caught the solitary soldier as he walked over to a woman waiting for the train. The soldier walked behind the woman and embraced her. The waiting woman didn't flinch. It was if she knew he was about to join her or that she was so wrapped up in the moment, she didn't notice him.

As the train came to a stop, passengers poured out into the station. Within a few minutes, the platform was empty except for a few staff, the woman and the soldier. The woman bowed her head, turn away from the soldier and walked away leaving the soldier standing there on his own. He walked over to a nearby bench seat, sat down and leant forward as if he was weeping.

"That was strange, did you see that, Rosie?"

"I did. It did seem a little odd. I expect there was perfectly reasonable explanation for it though. It's not a good idea to second guess these things."

"Yeah, I know that but who is he? Why is he here? And who was that woman? It don't make sense to me. Maybe he's a spy, maybe he's getting information from that woman. All seems a bit iffy to me."

Rose laughed. "You and your imagination, Jimmy. I bet it's totally innocent and I also bet it needs no help from us two gossip mongers".

The soldier stayed sat down for a while longer as if he was carrying the weight of the world on his shoulders. He seemed weakened by the woman he had just embraced as if the life had been sucked out of him. Was this the reason why he was at this station? Was this his new mission? A mission that only he could carry out. Maybe that's why he was alone. Only time would tell.

Jimmy was troubled. Not because of the strange actions of the soldier but more because he didn't quite seem to fit into the surroundings. There was something very odd about him. Even though there was a war on, Church Street was doing it's best to keep the Christmas spirit alive. As most places around town, things appeared cheerful and festive. That was the British way, keep smiling and knickers to Hitler. Christmas must go on. But there was a air of sadness around the soldier. It was if everything around him was in a shade of grey that was impossible for Jimmy to understand. Jimmy's wise ways of the world, or at least London, made him very aware of anything out of the ordinary. And this soldier was standing out more than anything or anyone he'd ever seen. But for now, he wouldn't say or do anything. He knew it would upset Rosie and that would kill him. Best just keep an eye out and make sure nothing happens.

There was another concern in the back of Jimmy's mind. Every time he looked at the soldier, he couldn't help but feel for the families of those lost in the war. He knew so many that had been touched by tragedy. In fact the whole country was in the same boat. Everyone knew someone who wouldn't be coming home but as long as everybody stuck together, he knew the losses wouldn't be in vain.

Still, he stared across at the soldier. For a brief moment, his previous thoughts of suspicion disappeared only to be replaced by sorrow and a want to go over and ask if he was OK. He knew if he did, he would get it in the neck from Rosie so he turned his attentions back to his news stand. After all, Christmas was on it's way and a crust had to be earned.

Mr Crispin had just about put the finishing touches to the tree. It truly was the shining light in the darkness. He had covered the branches with all sorts of ornaments and garlands. At the top, was a bright golden star that glinted in the sunlight that poured through the glass panes of the roof.

He stood back and admired his work. In true Mr Crispin style, he muttered "About bloody time!" In his strong northern accent. Although he could always find something to moan at, he was a kind and thoughtful man at heart, Many said his moaning was just a ruse to bolster his authority around the station. But everyone could see through it.

He gazed around the station, everything was normal. Nothing to get too concerned about so time to retire to his office for a well earned cup of tea.

CHAPTER THREE

LIFE GOES ON

The cold, dark winter evening once again was upon Church Street. It was the time that all Londoners dreaded. Night attacks from the Luftwaffe were a regular occurrence but the past few weeks, the raids had been coming earlier and earlier.

The air raids started back in July of that year, coming mostly at night when they were harder to spot by the Spitfires and Hurricanes of the Royal Air Force. But it wasn't just London being targeted, the Southern and Eastern coasts were also targets. In fact, ports all around the British Isles were being targeted. However, since October, the air raids were not restricted to night time attacks.

The Station was still fairly busy with the evening trains returning passengers in and out of the city although many of the traders were closing for the day. Best to get out of the open before the nightly raids begin. Although, the underground station provided protection for people, the traders also needed to protect their trade stands as best as possible. After all, after the bombs, life had to go on.

Jimmy had just packed away his news stand and wandered over to the flower stall. Rose was also packing up for the day. She tended to stay open as long as possible to try to catch the commuters on their way home who maybe tempted to buy a bunch for their wives and girlfriends. But business had been slowing down lately, especially with the earlier bombing runs.

"Are you ready for home, Rosie? I'll walk you back, make sure you get back safe."

Rosie smiled at Jimmy's concern for her. "I will be in a few minutes Jimmy, I just need to get the last of the flowers in, cover up and then lock away the cart."

The station gave the traders a secure area to lock away their stands. Although they all paid Mr Crispin tuppence a week for the privilege, it saved the hassle of lugging everything home each day. It also kept their goods safe from any light fingers. Although the communities were like big families and trusted each other, there was always the chancers who would try to nick anything that wasn't nailed down.

Rose finished lashing down the tarpaulin on the cart and Jimmy walked around to the cart handles to push it in to the lock-up when suddenly the air-raid warning began wailing.

"Bloody hell, Hitler's getting earlier and earlier, that man needs to get a hobby. C'mon Rosie, down the tube."

Jimmy grabbed Rose's hand and they ran to the stairs that led to the underground platform. Down in the underground, people sat waiting for the imminent bangs to begin. Old bunk beds lined the walls of the platform. Although they were meant to be for ticket owners, they were always given up for the old, lame and children. Church Street always looked after it's own.

For the next hour, bombs could be heard exploding in the distance. It seemed that the station wasn't in the flightpath of the swarm of bombers that night. Still, you could never be sure, knowing the Luftwaffe, one of them could have split off from the pack looking for an unsuspecting target. But for the time being, the inhabitants of Church Street Underground were thankful for small mercies. But never far from the mind of Jimmy and Rosie, was the suffering and tragedy that was taking place at that very moment just a short distance away from them. One unfortunate pub had taken a direct hit as the attack had begun. A few defiant punters were still inside along with the Landlord and his family.

Chapter 3

Nobody survived. A few streets away, a gas main was ruptured causing a fireball that ripped through an entire terrace block. Mercifully, the families had been evacuated to a nearby shelter and that particular casualty list consisted merely of bricks and mortar. But although, in this case, lives were not lost, they certainly were devastated. It would take many months, in some cases years before the damage was fully repaired. These traumatic stories were being told all over the capital during this evening. Every evening was the same.

Within a few hours, the bombing had ceased, the skies were now silent and the all clear was, once again, sounded. People started to emerge from their shelters to clean up the mess left by the raid, or in many cases to gather up what was left of their possessions. Rose and Jimmy ascended the stairs back into the main station. There was still the matter of securing the flower cart for the night and Rose had no intention of holding Jimmy back in the station for any longer.

"Jimmy, I need to finish here. Go home. I'll be fine now."

"No way, I'll hold on and give you a hand." Jimmy was very uncomfortable leaving Rose on her own.

"You're very sweet, but I'll be fine. Beside, I only live a few doors away. Nothing is going to happen to me walking 50 yards. Please Jimmy, I would feel better if you got off home."

Jimmy reluctantly agreed, said goodnight and wandered off leaving Rose to finish packing away. As she finally bolted shut the lock-up, she noticed that the soldier was still sat on the same bench from earlier. Had he been there during the raid? Why was he still at the station? She walked across to him. As she got closer she noticed that he was crying. She sat on the bench beside him.

Hello, are you OK?" It seemed he didn't hear the question. "Is there anything I can do?" Again, no answer. Ah well, she thought, I tried. She got up and began to walk away.

The soldier quietly spoke. "I feel their pain."

Rose stopped in her tracks and turned back to the soldier.

"Whose pain, love?"

"Them, out there. Those that have just been hurt and that have just died." The soldier's eyes remained fixed on a point directly in front of him. "Why can't they stop?"

Rose was confused, she couldn't make out what the soldier was talking about. As far as she knew he hadn't left the station all day, how did he know who had been hurt? "Is there someone you can talk to love? Where do you live? "

The soldier stood up and turned to Rose. "Thank you." He turned and walked out of the station leaving Rose bewildered.

The following morning greeted London with bright sunshine which shone strongly through the roof glass panels of Church Street warming the platforms below. For the station, life went on as normal. Unlike so many others in London, there was no rubble to clear away, no windows to repair, no searches to be carried out for missing people, just business as usual. Mr Crispin, looked around the daily hum-drum of the station and thanked God that it was so. But he knew deep in his heart it was just a matter of time before the stations luck would turn.

Rose and Jimmy were busy with their stalls. Jimmy's headlines were dominated by the Kings Head pub that was bombed the night before. Fifteen had died in the blast and countless more had been injured in the vicinity. Those poor souls, dying just because they were in the wrong place at the wrong time. The Great British resilience was not something which was apparent this morning around the remains of the pub. Only sadness and grieving.

Jimmy wandered over to Rose. She could see he wasn't his normal chipper self. He had a copy of the newspaper in his hand. She didn't have to ask what was bothering him.

"Did you know anyone in that pub?" She asked.

"No, no one. But I feel as if I did. It's really strange, I've never felt so sad for people I didn't know. I know the war effects us all but it feels as though I've just lost my family".

"That's not strange Jimmy, that just tells me you have a big heart and you care for people. You always have. Try not to beat yourself up about it. There's nothing any of us could've done to stop what happened." She put her hand tenderly on his arm. "You're a good man Jimmy but we have to go on. We still need to take care of what we have,"

Rose always knew what to say to bring Jimmy back to earth.

But something was bothering her, the conversation with the soldier kept running itself over and over in her head.

"Jimmy, when you left last night I saw that soldier. It looked like he had stayed up here when the bombs were falling. What was strange is that he said something similar to you. He said he felt their pain. What do you suppose he meant by that?"

Jimmy was concerned. "That's strange, when I left last night, there was only me and you here. I didn't see the soldier. How did he get in here?"

"I'm sure he didn't mean any harm but he was very sad. Maybe he wandered in when I was putting the cart away. Maybe that's what he meant, maybe he had seen it happen. The pub, I mean."

Jimmy wasn't sure. "Maybe, I'd still like to know who he is though. You know, just to make sure. He's probably well meaning and very nice but I couldn't forgive myself if anything happened. If he comes back, I'll have a quiet chat with him."

For a second Rose wondered if Jimmy's motives were more out of jealousy rather than curiosity. But she dismissed them. After all, emotions were running high after last night. She tried to reassure him.

"I know he didn't mean any harm. He just seemed sad. Besides, it didn't seem like he had any interest in the likes of us."

Jimmy backed down a little "Well, OK but I'll keep my eye on him if he comes back."

Indeed, he would be back. Church Street Station was the curse of Rifleman William Snow. He would contunue to visit the station as long as his comfort was needed there. Like Rose and Jimmy, he had no idea of why or how he got there. He just knew this is where he had to be and that's the way it was. But why was he no longer in France? As far as he knew, the war was still raging there but things seemed different. Soldiers were dressed differently, in fact everybody seemed to be dressed differently. The world had seemed to change in his time away. He knew something was wrong but simply had no answers to his questions. He just knew he had to be here, in this place, in this time. Time would reveal the mystery but only when it needed to.

CHAPTER FOUR

THE BATTLE WITHIN

Rifleman William Snow still didn't understand why he was at the station. All he knew is he had an overwhelming urge to comfort those who needed it. He had seen the pain and sacrifice of the battlefield and understood from a soldiers eyes. In fact the memories of 1916 never left his mind. But comforting the families, the lovers, the friends, those who had no control of what was happening to their loved ones was almost too much to bear. They were innocent, there were no choices, just the pain of having to deal with the enormous grief that was thrust upon them. But why him? Why did he feel the way he did and how did he get there? There was no explanation, just questions.

His last memory was the offensive on 31st August 1916 at Delville Wood. History would know this as the prelude to the Battle of Guillemont, one of the final offensives of the Somme campaign, which took place just a few days after. However, Delville Wood was subjected to intense German shelling which reduced the wood to nothing more than splinters before the counter-offensive to retake the wood was launched. William could remember the whistles in the trenches and then running forward on that day but nothing after that. Just standing on the station wanting to comfort others. No other memory in between existed.

But a strange thing had happened. A young woman had spoken to him. The only person that had spoken to him. That was something else that was bothering him. He was being ignored by everybody, even those who he comforted. It was if they didn't know he was there. But she was different, So much compassion and tenderness. She also seemed very wise above her years. But when she spoke to him he was feeling the pain of many that had just died very near to the station. The pain was overwhelming. It was if he saw all of their final moments all at the same time. Why would he bear such a curse? He felt very confused and afraid and couldn't help but cry for all of those people. But after the young woman spoke to him, the pain seemed to subside. Maybe she knew the answers to his questions.

For the time being though, he was back on Platform 1 waiting for another train. He didn't know anyone who was going to come in on the train but he just knew he needed to be there. He felt so tired though, he needed to sit down. As he sat on the bench on the platform, he stared down the track, his mind wandering back to France. He could see his friends falling as he ran forward, there was so much noise from the German guns, so much confusion but then the memories stopped. Nothing! Just this station,, just a knowing that he had to be there.

Mary Thompson walked on to the station with young Jack in tow. Jack was excited as he had not seen dad for almost a year now. Mary was nervous as she hadn't heard from her husband, Harry for over a month now. He had been in action in North Africa and, understandably, getting letters to home were not easy. She knew that. But she also knew that no news was good news so her hope and optimism remained. They walked past William Snow who was still sat on the bench and stood by the edge of the platform. In the distance, they could hear the inbound train whistling, announcing its arrival. Then within a few seconds the front of the green locomotive appeared slowing all of the time. The train stopped against the buffers of the platform and almost immediately, passengers began to pour out of the many carriage doors. Mary and Jack frantically searched along the platform hoping that Harry would show. Mary's heart began to sink as the dread crept back in. She looked down at Jack wondering what she was going to say to him when all of a sudden he let go of her hand and sprinted away. She looked up and saw the figure of a soldier at the other end of the train staring back at them. Jack ran straight at him and into a desperate hug. Dad was home.

Just a few feet away from the reuniting family stood Joan Matthers. She was waiting for her brother, Stephen to return on the same train. She never noticed the arms of William Snow embracing her, nor did she feel his tears as they fell on to her. She knew Stephen wasn't coming home. She could feel it. But something was giving her peace, she couldn't explain it but through her sadness, she simply turned away from William and walked off the platform. Her heart was broken, she wept as she walked away but still the peace was there. Unexplainable peace. She knew Stephen was gone, she didn't know when or how, there had been no letter yet from the army but she also knew he was OK wherever he was. Her mother and father would not be as calm but she thought that she could help them. She would be their strength.

Back on the platform, the grief of the loss of Stephen overwhelmed William. He wanted to scream out but couldn't find the strength, His emotions screamed out and he just wanted someone to comfort him and take away the pain. He felt weak and needed to sit. He found his bench and slumped down with his head in his hands trying to suppress the intense sadness, He wished the young woman would help him. He somehow knew she could take the pain away. He didn't know how, he just knew she could.

Jimmy had gone about his business in a quiet manner this morning. From all of the comings and goings on the platforms he could tell that it was going to be one of those days. He had already seen too many tears for one day and he really didn't want to add to anyone's distress. Thankfully, there was also a good helping of joy around too. There were plenty of families being reunited for Christmas such as Harry, Mary and Jack. He watched as they walked happily out of the station. Of course, with the night time raids it was going to be out of the frying pan and into the fire unless there were plans to escape the city. He hoped so.

The Spirit of Christmas 1940

The morning's trade had been busy for both Jimmy and Rose. Along with the extra passengers provided by the war, it was still business as usual. The usual commuters were still coming in and going out to their normal places of work regardless of the disruptions caused by the Luftwaffe. It was evident that the British spirit could not and would not be dented. Even in the station, business carried on as usual.

Just by the main ticket office was a bustling tea room, Sally's Cafe. This was one room that was busy from dawn till dusk. The proprietor, Sally Crispin was the daughter of the Station manager. A hard working but somewhat absent minded, cheerful young woman. She was cursed with being a little accident prone but always someone you could count on to lift your spirits. Mr Crispin was happy that Sally was close by at work. It meant that he knew she was safe and he could keep a fathers eye on her. He also knew that she was very much her own woman and she was the one member of staff in the station he couldn't give orders to. In fact, it was Sally that wanted to work at the station to keep her eye on her dad.

She would always make sure that the station staff and workers on the platforms were plied with tea throughout the day. They say Great Britain was built on a cup of tea and who was Sally to argue. She walked out of the front of the cafe, she had a cigarette hanging out of her mouth and was wearing a head scarf tightly bound over a nest of curlers, all of which hiding her real stunning beauty, but she wasn't bothered.

"Oi, Dad, come and get your brew, it's been here 10 minutes and it's getting cold." She yelled at the top of her voice. Everyone nearby stopped dead in their tracks at the sudden tea announcement. She turned and walked back into the cafe without a thought for the disruption she had just caused. Mr Crispin, walked across to the cafe red-faced but obedient. He certainly wasn't going to say anything to her for her recent scream, it would be a fate worse than death. Besides, the people in the vicinity only found it amusing including Rose and Jimmy, who was doubled up laughing at what had just happened. Only Sally could scream at the great Mr Crispin and get away with it.

As Mr Crispin walked into the cafe, he saw the reason for Sally's indiscretion. She was flying around the cafe, clearing and taking orders like a Blue Bottle Fly. He smiled at her and walked over to his mug of tea on the counter. She was a hard worker, sometimes she would take on a little too much, like now, but she wouldn't stop. She didn't take any nonsense from anybody, any customer, her dad, even the police watched their step when going in for a brew but she was very much loved and could always be relied upon.

Like Rose, in these times, she had no room for romance or going out and having fun. There was a war on and everyone had to do their bit as far as she was concerned. Any advances from the passing servicemen were normally met with unpleasant actions such as a quick witted and direct word or even, as in one instance, a cup of tea over the head. She had no time for that rubbish. But for now, she would bumble about her cafe and make sure everyone was taken care of.

Out on the station, Rosie had noticed the soldier sitting on the bench by Platform 1. He looked sad, which was how he always seemed to her. Jimmy had closed his stall for a while and disappeared to take advantage of another of his dodgy deals. He would often disappear like this but nobody minded as the deals he made eased the burden on the local community while rationing was gripping everyone.

Rose got up and wandered across to the soldier. It was more curiosity that drove her to go over to speak to him but nevertheless, she felt it was something she had to do.

As she approached the bench, the soldier seemed away with his thoughts. He seemed completely unaware Rose was walking towards him as if something was dominating his thought. Rose sat down and looked at him with a smile. She noticed that his skin seemed very pale and clammy and a little gray as if fear had scared all of the colour out of him.

"Are you OK? I couldn't help noticing that you were here again. Do you need any help?"

The soldier looked up at Rose, there was no expression, just blankness. The soldier spoke.

"I don't know. I can't make sense of anything. All I know is, I have to stay here until the all of the sadness is gone."

Rose looked bewildered. "I don't understand love, what sadness? Do you mean from people you know? I've noticed that you've comforted some people, Are they friends of yours? Are you expecting anybody else to come?

"No, I don't know them. I don't know anybody here. I don't know why I've been sent here, All I know is I have to try to take their pain away."

Rose was really getting confused now. "I don't know what you mean love. Who sent you here?"

"I don't know. All I can remember was fighting, we went over the top, I was running across a field and then I was here. I don't know how, I don't know why, it just happened. I can't remember anything else. But I do know I have a job to do here, I feel it. When I see the families waiting for the ones coming home, I can see the ones that are going to be sad and I try to take their pain away. But when I do, I feel their pain. It hurts so much. I wish I could understand what's happening to me. How is it you can see me and nobody else can?"

"Other people do see you love. My friend Jimmy has seen you about too. I'm sure there are others. What's your name?"

"William, William Snow."

"Pleased to meet you William. My name is Rose. Now you have a friend here. Where do you live William?"

William got up to leave. "I'm sorry Rose, I have to go" He looked uncomfortable at the question and clearly didn't want to answer, or was it he couldn't answer.

"That's OK, I work here everyday if you need to talk about anything. Take care of yourself William."

William turned and walked away. She watched him walk out of the station and thought about what he had just said to her. She couldn't make any sense of it. Had something happened to him which made him lose his memory? Was he just confused? Whatever was the matter she knew he needed a friend and some help. There was something about him that didn't quite fit in to place. She didn't know what it was, but there was something.

She walked back over to her flower stall still in deep thought. Jimmy had arrived back from his business dealings and was getting ready to get on with his normal business when he noticed Rose by her stall. He noticed straight away that she was looking unusual, something was troubling her. He walked over to her.

"Are you OK, Rosie?"

Rose suddenly snapped out of her deep thought, turned to Jimmy and smiled. "Yes, fine, sorry I was just thinking. I've just had a very weird conversation with that soldier." She went on to explain the events that had happened between William and her. Like Rose, Jimmy couldn't make any sense of William either. Despite the mysteries, there was a thought that Rose could not dismiss. What on earth had happened to William. Regardless of his reasons for being here, something very bad had happened to him and it was tearing him apart. There was one thing clear, what ever it was, he also didn't understand it.

He was suffering, not physically but certainly in his mind. His pain appeared similar to the look of the broken men arriving daily on the trains from Europe. Those men had seen death and suffering on a massive scale and no matter what, those injuries would never leave them. They could not be healed. In fact, they were cursed to fight this illness for the rest of their lives. They, like William were now fighting the battle within.

CHAPTER FIVE

DELVILLE WOOD

It was a particularly quiet night at Church Street, the nightly air raids had passed some distance away and the station was relieved to be able to close down in relatively normal circumstance. Everybody had returned home for the night and the station was now empty and at peace, apart from one. William Snow.

William was sat on the bench by Platform 1. He didn't notice the cold, winter air creeping in around him. In fact, physically, he felt very little anymore. Only the pain in his mind remained.

His thoughts drifted back to days gone by in a hope that an answer could be found somewhere in his memory. Much of his past, he could remember with absolute clarity. He could remember his parents, going to school, joining up with his friends in Stafford. He remembered sailing out of Southampton to go across to France. He could remember the excitement of wanting to be a hero and being part of the British Army. The good guys. He didn't know what the future held but he wanted to be part of it. It was his duty.

He had joined the 11th Battalion. The Rifle Brigade (The Prince Consorts Own) in 1914. But it wasn't until July the following year before he would depart for France, landing at Boulogne-sur-Mer ready for service on the Western Front. It had been a good year before the Battalion departed, enjoying the Hampshire countryside with his fellow soldiers between the basic training. He had enjoyed the training, finding it a lot of fun but being a keen footballer from Smethwick in Staffordshire, he was naturally fit and found the physical training fairly easy.

By the summer of 1915, they were getting impatient to get across to France and do their bit. Of course, there was a bit of apprehension but also so much excitement. They were going, and that was that. But the reality of the trenches very quickly took hold and morale, although covered by humour of the troops, started to be affected.

William was one of the eldest members of his platoon even though he was just 21 himself. Most were barely old enough to be called adults. 17, 18, 19, just boys. William being in his twenties was considered the one that the rest could turn to. Although he would stay a Rifleman, he was respected as if he was a Non- Commissioned Officer. He was OK with this, it was a good distraction to be able to help his guys out even if it was just a comforting chat.

The next year would prove a test for William as the 11th Battalion went from battle to battle and the lads he came out with got fewer and fewer. But still, he tried to be the one who could be relied upon to steady the nerves. That was his gift, the calm in the storm. A gift that would be needed and strongly tested as the Battle for the Somme raged.

In July 1916, the Battalion was in action on the run up to the third attack on the Somme. They were situated at a piece of woodland not far from Longueval called Delville Wood. During mid-July, the South African forces had taken the wood in a very costly battle and now held the position. However, there had been numerous counter-offensives from the German war machine to retake it. The lush forest of Beech and Hornbeam had been reduced to a quagmire of mud after the constant artillery bombardments and the beautiful French copse was no more. The First World War took no prisoners of nature.

The to-ing and fro-ing of counter offensives continued through to the end of August when a large push through was ordered for the 31st. The 11th was just one of the battalions who would attack the German line to finish that particular campaign.

Once again, William was steadying his fellow troops as he had done before. Some were so scared of the upcoming battle they were vomiting with worry. William made sure he would get to as many as he could to comfort them with his humour and inner strength as the NCO's checked on the ammunition and kit of the men. The sergeants were pleased to have William within the platoon, they knew they didn't need to worry about him, in fact they needed him as much as any corporal. His officers had already recommended him up the chain of command for promotion but the constant tasking of the battalion had meant any such things were not a priority for the time being.

The men were formed up in the trenches, ready to storm the enemy positions. The waiting was always the worst bit. It was the fever that attacked the mind, the reason for fear. The illness didn't last long as the orders came down the line to prepare to attack. They turned and tensed themselves. The pause seemed like an eternity, hearts were pounding, hands were trembling. The whistles blew, William scrambled to the top and began to run forward. The few hundred yards between the lines erupted with the dirt being thrown up from machine gun fire and shells. He could see men falling on both sides but he couldn't stop. He had to keep going, if he stopped then what would the young ones think, the ones he had tried to give courage to? He could see the other side, he could see the German troops. He let out a war cry as he charged forward then... Nothing. The memories were gone.

William opened his eyes, he was back on the station. He felt cold. Not because of the Winter weather but because of the fear that was engulfing him. Was this shellshock? Maybe whatever happened on that day had been so horrific that his mind had blanked it out. Had something knocked him senseless? Maybe he was... No, that was impossible. He dismissed the thought. There had to be some plausible reason as to why he could remember nothing else since the battle.

All he knew that he was on a Railway station in London giving comfort to those who had lost their loved ones, taking away their pain with a simple touch. For a moment, he wondered if this was indeed a curse or had he been given a gift to help others in ways nobody else could? If it was a gift, why did it cause him so much pain. He felt such as sense of loss for all of those he comforted even though he didn't know who they were. There were no answers, just questions.

N.B. *The real William Snow fell wounded on a counter-offensive on 31st August 1916 at Delville Wood. He died the following day of his wounds and was laid to rest at La Neuville Cemetery, Corbie, France shortly after. The description of the battle is an interpretation based on facts and research along with a degree of artistic licence purely for the purpose of this book. Any similarities to any person, living or deceased outside of this novel is purely coincidental.*

They shall not grow old as we that are left grow old. Age shall not weary them, nor the years condemn.

At the going down of the Sun and in the morning, we will remember them.

CHAPTER SIX

DECK THE HALLS

The Christmas season was in full swing on Church Street Station, Mr Crispin had finally finished his mammoth task of adorning the station with decorations and there was an air of excitement in the faces of the normal commuters. Of course, Christmas was still a week away but, true to the normal British form, the spirit was thriving.

Rose's gaze and ears were firmly fixed on the group of children singing carols by the cafe. The local school was on an early Christmas break thanks to a recent raid by the Luftwaffe. Thankfully, being a night raid, only bricks and mortar was damaged. Nonetheless, it gave an early holiday for the kids who jumped on the chance to sing for a few pennies. Rose was loving it. She had a big soft spot for the traditions. She enjoyed even more, the smells from the Christmas trees and wreaths on her stall. It was a nice change from all of the attention on the war.

But the Christmas trees and holly wreaths weren't the only smells hanging around the station. There was something romantic and exhilarating about the smells of the locomotives coming in and going out of the station. The steam engines left a powerful smell of coal and oil which, although not the healthiest of aromas, was certainly something to savor. Yes, it was Christmas at Church Street Station.

Rose was singing along cheerfully to the carols when she noticed William sitting on the bench by Platform 1 again. She picked up a white rose from her stall and walked over to him.

"Good morning William, waiting for somebody?" She said with a naughty smile.

"No, not at the moment, I'm just sitting here thinking. I wanted to say thank you for speaking to me the other day. You're the first person who had spoken to me since... well, a long time."

Rose looked puzzled. "How long? I mean, I'm not even sure where you're from."

"I'm not sure, I've been trying to work it out but still nothing is making sense to me. I think I have an idea but it's impossible. I mean really impossible. Maybe it's best that we don't know for the time being. It's scaring the hell out of me to face up what I'm thinking but.. Ah, forget it. It'll work itself out."

"OK, you take your time. Anyway I've got a present for you." She placed the rose into a lapel hole on his jacket "There you, go."

William looked surprised, "What's that for?"

"Oh, just to cheer you up a bit. It looks like you could do with it. "

"Rose, can I ask you something weird? What do you think happens when somebody dies? Do you believe in Heaven and hell or do you think we go on to another life?

The question startled Rose. In a moment a bizarre thought crossed her mind but was very quickly dismissed as madness.

"I don't know really, My dad raised me to believe in the Bible as a Christian but I suppose I'm like everyone else, Wondering what the truth is. I suppose it's something that we will only know when the time comes. Why do you ask"

"I wish I could tell you. It's just something which I've been thinking about. As I said, I've got a lot of questions that I can't find the answer to."

"William, what's going on. Where are you going with all of this?"

"I honestly don't know. I'm trying to find the answers as to why I'm here but nothing is making sense to me.."

William wanted to get Rose to tell him the answers but was afraid to scare her off. He thought maybe if he started with what he knew, it may help.

"Rose, what would you say if I told you I was born in 1894"

Rose felt very uncomfortable all of a sudden. It was if she didn't want to know where this was leading.

"Um, I would say you look really young for a man of forty six. But you're clearly not forty six. You can only be in your early twenties,"

"My last memory was in France in 1916. I can't remember anything else until I found myself here not so long ago, waiting to help people in pain on this station. ".

"OK, you're scaring me now William, what you're saying is impossible, There's got to be a simple reason to why you think this. Maybe you had a bang on the head and have lost your memory, your true memory. Yes, I bet that's all it is. The mind can do funny things when you've hurt yourself. That would explain why you can't remember and why you think you were in France and why you think your as old as you think you are. I bet you're only helping people simply because you're a nice person"

Rose new she was desperately fighting to find a rational answer, she was forcing a thought out of her head. Surely it wasn't possible. She couldn't bring herself to entertain the fact that he was... No, she couldn't even think it. It was a bang on the head. That's the only answer, she thought. The only thing that made sense. Rose was drifting away in thought, self arguing the facts.

"Rose, are you OK?"

"Yes, I'm fine. I don't know what to say. I think I just need to think about this for a bit, sorry William, I'll see you later."

Rose had to walk away. She had to think. William's heart sank. He had opened up to someone who he thought would listen and she had walked away. Was he really going mad or was it like Rose said. Maybe he did have a bang on the head, it would make sense if only his memories weren't so clear. Just let her go, he thought. It was an awful lot to take in. He would give her time.

The evening was creeping in at Church Street. Once again, the usual trade was coming to an end and the station was starting to empty itself of its daily hustle and bustle. As usual, Rose and Jimmy were packing up their business and preparing to go home. Rose was still full of thought from the days events with William. She wanted to believe and make sense of it all but still, those questions still could not be answered.

She looked around the station, William was nowhere to be seen. She was pleased of that for the time being, it relieved the tension a little and prevented an awkwardness she really didn't want to feel with him around.

Jimmy had been keeping an eye on her all afternoon. He had noticed that something wasn't quite right but had refrained from saying anything, he didn't want to add to her worries. If she wanted to talk, all she needed to do was ask. He would leave things, at least for the time being. There was one thing he was positive of though, the cause of Rose's thoughts was that damn soldier. He would find a chance to have a word with him while Rose wasn't about. But for now he would just keep an eye on her.

He walked across to Rose with a cheerful look so she wouldn't be suspicious of him.

"Oi Rosie, I'm off to the Swan for a pint, do you fancy joining me for one before we go home?"

Rose was about to answer when the air raid sirens started to wail. Jimmy looked up "That knackers that, then. C'mon, down the tube" They walked across to the subway entrance, no rush needed, There was always a few minutes before anything happened.

They reached the top of the stairs and began the long decent to the underground platforms.

"I'm getting fed up of these raids. All they ever do is kill innocent people and destroy there..." Jimmy was cut off mid sentence with a blinding flash of light as the station erupted. For a moment he could hear nothing, then intense noise from the explosion, then just ringing in his head. The shock-wave from the blasted lifted them both off their feet and threw them into different directions.

It seemed an eternity of unconsciousness. Almost peaceful, oblivious to the chaos going on outside his mind. He wanted to stay in the calm, he felt safe there but something was trying to break in. Something that wouldn't let him stay in the peace.

Only a few seconds had passed when he opened his eyes gagging on the mixture of dust and smoke charging down the stairway. He coughed over and over desperately trying to clear his airway and get his mind focused.

And then reality hit him, Rosie, where the hell was Rosie. She was with him but now she was gone. He got to his feet, his eyes were blurry with dust. He tried to make out what was going on but nothing was clear. He wiped his eyes, clearing some of the dust out. Although his sight was still blurry, he could make out a pile of rubble that was moving as if it had a life of its own. He frantically started clearing the debris away when his hand felt hair. His heart sank.

"Oh God, no. Rosie!" He dug at the brick and dirt till his fingers started bleeding calling her name over and over. He managed to get hold of her shoulders and pulled her free of the pile. She started to cough and opened her dust filled eyes.

"Bloody hell. I can't hear a damn thing!" She was shaken up but OK much to the relief of Jimmy who dropped to his knees.

"Thank God, Rosie, don't ever do that to me again."

Rosie smiled as she coughed "I'll try not to."

A bomb had gone clean through the roof of the station and partially exploded just as Rose and Jimmy had walked down the stairs. Thankfully only windows and the entrance to the subway were damaged and apart from a few cuts and bruises from the blasts shock-wave, nobody was hurt.

The all clear was finally sounded and Rose and Jimmy walked back up to the main station, Jimmy clutching Rose as if his life depended on her preservation. He was truly frightened for the first time in his life, not for himself but the thought that he could have lost Rose. The very thought that she could have been taken from him and she would never have known how he felt about her. Of course in reality, she knew very well but she always wanted him to open up first.

Rose saw the fear in his face and noticed his hands trembling.

"Jimmy, are you OK? You're shaking like a leaf. Surely that little bomb didn't scare you? Not my Jimmy."

He looked at her, a tear rolled down his cheek. "I'm OK, It's just seeing you in that pile of rubble scared me to death. I don't know what I would do if I lost you."

"Hey, I'm not going anywhere, a little bit of brick dust isn't going to slow me down." She was looking at the man she knew, the cockney confidence king who could sell ice to the Eskimos for a rich profit, the man who could talk his way out of the gates of hell, looking like a lost orphan, scared and vulnerable.

"All of these years I've known you Rose, I've never... Well, I haven't... Oh, you know what I mean. "

"No Jimmy, I don't know what you mean. What are you trying to say?"

"I love you damnit, I really love you"

"Language Jimmy" Rose was having a little fun trying to get his mind off the events from earlier. "I know you do. Why has it taken you so long to tell me?"

Because I'm a coward. Nothing terrifies me in this world quite like you."

Rose smiled at him, for the first time since she had known him, he was showing his heart. His true self. She hugged him and held on to him until a smile appeared on his face.

"Merry Christmas Jimmy."

CHAPTER SEVEN

LET THE BELLS RING OUT

It had been a few days since the station had been hit by the bomb and everything was returning to normal. The debris had been cleared away and the damage was under repair, or at least the best that could be done during the testing times. The damage to the station was considered minor and thus, unimportant. However, the staff and their families had all chipped in to get service back to normal.

Rose and Jimmy were back after their ordeal, albeit still wearing a few cuts and bruises but generally none the worse for wear. They were back to working on their stalls, as not working meant not eating. Rose had to feed her father and Jimmy was the sole provider for his family. Still, it was better to be busy than to be sitting around thinking about the past few days.

Although it was Christmas Eve, the war was still raging, A troop train was due in to Church Street that morning with soldiers returning form the North Africa Campaign which had begun earlier that month.

Families were already gathering in the station waiting for their loved ones. Many would be taken directly to the nearby hospitals to recover from their wounds, some would board the convoy of military truck parked at the station entrance to ferry some back to barracks ready to be reassigned. Some would be lucky enough to go home with their families for Christmas. Many would be taken to be prepared for burial. They would be carried from the train, through the station to the awaiting trucks. It was always a very moving occasion when these trains came in. Respect from the population in the station was absolute. Until the trucks left, there would be no trade, no train movement, just people stood in silence. Until then, people did their best to carry on as usual.

The one saving grace from the war was that there was to be a two day ceasefire of aerial operations between Great Britain and Germany. At least for two days, London would be safe from the Luftwaffe's aerial bombardments. A most welcome change of pace for Christmas. People could go to the pubs, or at least those that were still standing, to celebrate the festivities. Families could celebrate in peace and the streets could be walked safely.

Back in the station, Rose had just finished setting up her stall for the day. The colours of the flowers were definitely welcome with the drab repairs going on around the station. Her mind was a very confused place. On one hand, she had the feeling of love following the kiss between her and Jimmy, although she hadn't seen him since. On the other, she could not get William out of her mind. She still didn't know how she felt about him. He was nice to talk to even though he was very sad and he was definitely charming but something about him was wrong. That in itself leant to an air of forbidden attraction which she couldn't help. But it was now very clear that Jimmy would be her man. Nothing could get in the way of that. But why was she thinking such thoughts? There was no love with William, those feelings were for Jimmy alone.

She peered around to see if William was there. With the arrival of the troop train later, she was sure he would appear at some point. But she could not see him for the time being. Her train of thought was interrupted by a kiss on the cheek from the blushing Jimmy.

"Mornin' Rosie, here you go." He presented her with a rose he had just pinched from her cart. "How're you feelin' today? I haven't been able to sleep a wink since the other evening."

"Oh you daft old thing." Rosie smiled "I'm totally fine and very happy to see you back here." She accepted the flower and held it to her chest "Thank you."

Jimmy was feeling a little awkward. Everything had changed

since the bomb. He was no longer comfortable with Rose. Not in a bad way, but the hunt was over and all of a sudden he was faced with a different person. Of course it was still Rosie but the game had changed. He looked at her differently. She was so beautiful but he now had to be her man. For years he would show off as much as he could to impress her but now the Peacock was stripped of his plumage, now he had to show his true self, his heart and that was a different thing altogether. A much scarier thing.

"Now, you get back to your newspaper stand and earn some pennies and I might let you take me for a cup of tea later."

"Oh OK, just remember that train is coming in today. Best wait until the station has calmed down first. Hey, maybe we can go for a glass of beer in the Swan later, there's not going to be any planes out tonight."

"OK, I'll talk to my dad later and make sure he's OK first'"

At last, Rosie had agreed to go out on a date with him. Even though it was just in the Swan. The Swan was the small pub attached to the station. It was very much a locals pub but the commuters and passengers, especially the servicemen passing through were always welcome.

The Swan was run by a cantankerous old man, Stan Crispin, the older brother of the station manager, James. Stan liked nothing better than to moan about the war, about the rationing, the state of the streets, the youth, in fact anything at all was fair game. He, like his brother, was a stickler for discipline and tidiness. This was always evident when someone would walk in to his pub. Clean, tidy, organised and welcoming. Behind the bar, he would come across as miserable but the locals knew that was just the way he was and there was nothing meant by it. He was helped in his domain by his wife, Esther. She was completely different from her husband. Kind, caring, very friendly and had an infectious sense of humour. She never let Stan's miserable persona get the better of her. She would simply just ignore him with a smile and get on with her day without raising an eyebrow.

That was the Swan. Along with the cafe, they provided a community hub for Church Street Station. A place where life could be normal for a short time. A welcome pint of bitter or a nice cup of tea was the medicine which would invigorate the spirit no matter how hard times would get.

William Snow was sat on the bench by Platform 1 waiting for the incoming train. He knew the pain he would suffer before the day was through. Somehow, he knew today would be worse than before. He felt it in his heart, he could feel the sadness that surrounded this particular train even though it still had not arrived. He feared the pain more than the fear of the battlefield he once knew.

The questions of recent times had faded for the time being. These were thoughts for when times were quiet and peaceful. Times when no others needed help. That was not today.

Rose spotted him sat on the bench, She would not walk over to him for the moment, he was deep in thought and she felt he didn't want to be disturbed. Besides, she still felt awkwardness at the thought of speaking to him. What would she say? She hadn't seen him since she had walked away. Maybe there was a little guilt there, she thought. Best just leave him be for the time being.

The announcement of the arriving train came from a shriek from the steam powered locomotive as it slowed into the station. It had finally arrived. It stopped at Platform 1 and the doors to the carriages swung open. Almost straight away servicemen were pouring out on to the station. Those that had families waiting wore a look of excitement and relief and within minutes they were leaving, looking forward to having Christmas as a family. Other soldiers walked off the station with empty stares. They walked slow as if with no purpose seeing nothing around them. The soldiers who had been sent to meet them gathered them and helped them out of the station along with those who were injured. Men on crutches, armless, blind and some blindly insane.

A tear fell from Rose's eye as she watched the parade pass through the station. It was heartbreaking to see the broken men coming home from somewhere they should never have been. They should have been with their families or working on farms or in offices rather than getting shot at or blown up.

The station was respectfully silent as they moved out. No matter how many times these trains came through, nobody could become accustomed to the sadness they brought.

Within a few minutes, all that remained were families that were hopelessly waiting for their loved ones to emerge from the train. Instead, William walked amongst them stopping at each and embracing them for a short time and then moving to the next. The presence of William remained unnoticed by all on the station except Rose. As far as the heartbroken families were concerned, there was nothing or no-one, just a sense of peace. Rose stood rigid as the truth dawned on her. Everything he had said was making sense. William was a spirit. A spirit that had been sent to ease the suffering caused by the war. In this one moment she could see it. She couldn't believe what she was seeing but it was really happening in front of her eyes.

William moved from the families to where the coffins were being loaded on to the transport. He was looking exhausted and distraught. He placed a hand on to each coffin momentarily, again totally unnoticed by those there. Each coffin seemed to draw the energy from him more and more until finally he walked away back to his bench. As he reached it, he collapsed.

Rose ran over to him, why was nobody helping? Everybody was just walking past. Nobody could see him!

"William, are you OK love?"

William seemed almost unconscious and in a lot of pain. She placed a hand onto his shoulder. She could feel him trembling which again made her wonder about who he really was. Can spirits possess a physical body? Ghosts were meant to be see-through and scary but William felt very real. He was cold and seemed to be a different colour but one thing she was positive of, he was not frightening in any way. In fact, exactly the opposite, there was an overwhelming sense of peace that surrounding him. When she placed her hand on his shoulder, she felt that everything was going to be OK. Was this the feeling that those families felt when he was with them?

"I'm OK Rose, I just need to rest for a while. Go back to your stall, I'll be fine."

"William, I think we need to talk when you're feeling up to it." She knew why he was here. She also knew that he didn't and she would have to be the one that explained it to him. How do you tell somebody that they are dead and now a ghost, she thought. This was not the time for that conversation though.

He looked at her and smiled. He closed his eyes and seemed to drift off to sleep. Rose left him and walked back to her stall still wondering about the ghost soldier she was befriending, This was such a surreal situation. It was clear that he had been sent for a specific purpose. A very spiritual purpose. She believed that William had been chosen especially for this job. What kind of person was he during his life? He must have been kind and compassionate or was this some kind of punishment for something he did? No, that couldn't be it. He wore the uniform of a soldier. Soldiers were heroes. Maybe that was it, maybe God needed someone who was strong and who could be relied upon. Now that she was believing in William, more questions were being raised in her mind, She had to find some way of just accepting and not asking why so much. She did wonder though, why only she and Jimmy could see him. Were they part of all of this? Again, she dismissed the questions, she would just try to help him. He was all alone with this and she needed to help him in whatever way she could. But how was she going to explain all of this to Jimmy? He would never believe that William was a spirit. Jimmy believed in what he could see, certainly nothing that was supernatural. Maybe it would be kinder for him to just figure this out for himself like she'd had to. Besides, he would think she was mad and that could spoil everything that had started between them. She wasn't going to risk that.

The station was finally clearing from the troop train and things were slowly getting back to normal. Within no time at all, it was hard to imagine that such a sad event had occurred but the locals needed to find happiness when ever and where ever they could. Tomorrow was Christmas Day and there would be no bombing for at least two days. Church Street needed to embrace that. They needed these two days of happiness to remind them of hope in the midst of war.

Once James Crispin was sure that there was no one left from the Soldier train, he arranged for the carol singers to go out in to the station and spread a little festive cheer. Annoyingly, the Christmas tree had to be replaced after the recent bomb had decimated his pride and joy. Of course, replacing the tree was never going to be a problem but James Crispin took it personally, as if the Luftwaffe had purposely bombed the station just to destroy all of the work he had put in to it. The day after the bomb, Sally had brought in a new one. If she hadn't, the old man would be a pain in the neck until the new year, she thought. As soon as it had arrived, Mr Crispin was straight into action getting it decorated. It was so important for him to let his customers and staff know it was Christmas.

So Christmas was well under way. The tree was back, carols were being sung, peace had descended on the station and finally smiles and excitement was beginning to appear on peoples faces. William reminisced back to the Christmas before he went off to war when tales of the Christmas truce of 1914 were being told. That Christmas when troops left their trenches and walked across No-Man's Land to greet their enemies. Enemies that would become friends for a very short time, enemies that would become the opposition on the football field drawn out in the shell-holes and mud, enemies that would share the common bond of man for a short time to celebrate the birth of Christ. That particular Christmas would go down in history as a sign of hope and a message that peace to all men was very possible even though it only lasted a few short days. Still, it was a big moral boost for William's battalion as they left Southampton docks for France, anything was possible.

William would walk the streets that evening listening to those who celebrated, hoping that those who could not, were finding peace. Meanwhile, Rose and Jimmy made it to the Swan for a Christmas drink. The worries of recent times would be put aside for tonight and the spirit of Christmas 1940 could finally be enjoyed. The station would be empty on Christmas Day except for those who needed to perform essential tasks or those who simply had no other place to go.. Rose would be with her dad, Jimmy would be with his mum, brother and sister and the Crispins were having Christmas lunch behind the closed doors of the pub. William would spend his Christmas day on the platforms of Church Street station, alone and in thought. Maybe Chistmas day would be a day where he would find an answer to what was happening. He was a little sad that he wouldn't see Rose. She was the one sign of hope and joy that he could hold on to. In all of the confusion that he felt, he knew she was the calm in the storm.

He couldn't entertain the thought of falling for Rose, that in itself seemed impossible, even forbidden. But he did need her as a friend. She was his only friend.

CHAPTER EIGHT

CHRISTMAS DAY 1940

The sun shone brightly making the heavy frost sparkle diamond white in the crisp, morning air. The streets were full of people taking a Christmas morning walk and greeting each other with the traditional 'Merry Christmas'. Kids were playing with their new toys and there was a welcome feeling of peace and happiness.

It was a surreal sight, people celebrating Christmas day so warmly amidst the rubble and damage of the recent nightly bombings. It really was a testament to how happiness could still exist during times of hardship and suffering. This was the British spirit.

William stood at the entrance to the station looking out on to the street where Christmas was well under way. He felt no pain today, just quietness. At least quietness within, he felt calm as if nobody would suffer today. Of course, there were those spending Christmas without their loved ones, some mourning those lost and many sick and injured but he couldn't feel them today. It was a blessing. The quietness, however, was only within as he watched the hustle and bustle of the celebrations around him. He enjoyed the sound of a group of carol singers as they gave a rendition of 'God Rest Ye Merry Gentlemen'. He watched a young boy swooping around with a model wooden plane in his hand that his dad had made for him. As he ran, he made the sound of machine guns, pretending he was the RAF taking on the Luftwaffe. A couple of other lads were kicking a football around while others were just running around with their friends, keeping out of the way of their busy mothers preparing the Christmas day feast of Turkey and all the trimmings.

William remembered the Christmases back home in Stafford. They seemed different to what he could see today, they were more simple but happy all the same. He remembered the Christmas fruit cake that his mother, Jessie would make. He would love to taste the rum that was splashed into the mixture. He thought about the carols that he used to sing with his parents around the coal fire in the evening. It was always a really happy time.

Williams train of thought was interrupted by a familiar voice.

"Morning William." Rose had been out taking her morning walk and decided to pop by the station to see if William was around. "Morning Rose, Merry Christmas. What brings you down this way today? You should be at home with your family". Although he was asking through true concern, he was pleased she had come.

"Oh, I was just taking a walk. I thought I would check up on the station... And you." The comment startled Jimmy a little.

"There was no need, I'm fine. Besides, there's a strange feeling of peace here today. It's a nice change. You should be with your dad today, celebrate Christmas with him."

Rose sighed "Oh, he'll be sleeping most of the day. I'll just wake him when dinner is ready. He's fine. But I couldn't help thinking that you'd be here all day on your own, it doesn't seem right. Why don't you come home with me in the warm and have Christmas dinner with us?"

The invite was really tempting but he knew he couldn't leave the station. This was where he was meant to be. "I'd love to Rose but I must stay here. Don't ask me why, I just know that's what I have to do."

Rose knew he was right. He had to stay at the station. After all, she knew why he was on the station, she was the only one who knew, William included.. The loneliness and the mystery that surrounded William seemed a little chilling, especially today of all days. She wondered whether William had any relatives. She remembered that he had said that his home town was Stafford. His last memory was apparently 1916 which was only twenty four years earlier. It was very possible that his parents were still living, maybe even other family members that he could be unaware of. It was a very sad thought.

"I need to go back home and get lunch ready for dad but maybe

I could pop back later for a while and make sure you are OK. I expect a little company couldn't hurt you".

William smiled. "You don't have to do that but it is always nice to see you. But don't sacrifice your time at home just so you can make sure I'm OK, I'll be fine".

Rose smiled, turned and left. She had wanted to tell him the truth, but again she found an excuse, through Christmas day not to.

Once again, William was alone with his thoughts, But at least, today, they were of Christmas's gone by.

As the day progressed, Church Street slowly quietened, Over lunch time, the pubs that were still standing, opened their doors for a few brief hours allowing fathers, husbands and other male family members to get away from the mayhem of the busy kitchens and enjoy a couple of pints. One such man had been Jimmy. His mother actually told him to get out of the house and go to the pub as he had proved little more than useless since he had got up. Playing with his Christmas excited siblings and getting under his mothers feet had just proved too much, so he was banished from the house for a couple of hours. He would have a pint or two and then pop around to Rose to wish her a merry Christmas. He had received a letter in the post on Christmas eve and needed to tell her about it's contents but this was not a subject to be discussed until after the festive season. He was being called up for service in the RAF and would be leaving for basic training within a few weeks.

Most men between the age of 19 and 27 were conscripted in to either the army or the RAF during 1940 unless they were already working for the war effort or were unable to fight because of a physical problem. He had thought that he had been overlooked and had escaped the call up as most eligible men in his area had already been drafted earlier in the year. The letter had come out of the blue and a shock to his mother. But the family had decided to make the best of the Christmas time and put the thoughts of the call up and war out of their minds for the time being.

He knew Rose would be upset. They had been getting on really well recently and he had finally told her how he felt. Something which had taken an awful lot of courage. But before they had the chance to really get to know each other and start courting properly, he was leaving for the war. It was going to be tough on them both but he wasn't worried about himself, just Rose. He would have a good Christmas and tell her after. Today he would give her the gift he had put aside for her since the summer. Perfumes in such times were an extravagant luxury and were very hard to come by since the country had been gripped by rationing. Through a business acquaintance, he had managed to get his hands on a bottle which had found its way into his possession through unorthodox methods. He knew it was the only present she would get as she was an only child and her father was housebound. He would make sure that she had a reason to smile on Christmas day.

As the cold evening sky drew in, Church Street was silent. The day's celebrations had taken their toll on the population who were now sleeping off copious amounts of Christmas cheer, or celebrating quietly within the confines of their homes. It was hard to imagine that amidst the Christmas celebrations, there was a war on. For the best part of six months Great Britain had been subjected to relentless bombings and aerial battles from the Luftwaffe reducing many cities to rubble. The capital had certainly taken a huge brunt of the assault leaving the once bustling metropolis in ruins. Still, the past day or two had been a very welcome change. At least the occupants could walk the streets in relative safety.

Jimmy was walking off his day on the quiet streets. After he left the pub he had stopped off at Rose's house. He had knocked several times but there had been no answer. She had probably popped out to see relatives, he thought. While he was out walking, he would pop around and say hello. She should be back home now,

As he approached Rose's house he noticed all of the lights were off. It was still early evening, surely she wouldn't be in bed already. He decided not to disturb her just in case and walked on towards the station. He would check up on things there just in case any opportunists had visited and taken advantage of the lack of personnel. He was very aware of the dodgier side of London, especially as he had dealings with that side himself. But home was home and he felt a duty to keep an eye on things.

The station doors were open allowing people to take shelter if needed although the stalls, businesses and offices were all securely locked up. At least he could satisfy himself that all was well.

As he walked around the empty station he could hear voices. He wandered towards platform one and spotted Rose sat on the bench with that soldier who had been hanging around recently. His heart sank. All of a sudden, he had the feeling of jealousy and being betrayed. He had opened his heart to Rose and told her how he felt. Something which didn't come very easy to the cockney lad. He couldn't believe he had been so gullible. He knew that soldier was no good, this proved it. He was trying to move in on her, and it looked like she would rather be here. Was this where she was this afternoon? He couldn't think straight, he turned and walked out of the station and back towards home. On his way home he entertained the thought that maybe it was all innocent and she was just being Rose, caring for others. But on Christmas day? The one day when he expected to see her. Maybe he was reading too much into the relationship between them. He would know tomorrow when the station reopened.

A little earlier in the evening, Rose had finished cleaning up after having Christmas dinner with her dad, got him settled down to bed and finally relaxed in her armchair listening to the radio broadcast. She was surprised Jimmy hadn't come around to say hello. Perhaps he was busy with his family at home. She knew that he was the bread winner and the whole family looked to him as the man of the house. He had been looking out for them for so long that it was just naturally how things were done. He never complained or questioned it, he was a good man. Maybe one day, she would be part of that particular family, she hoped. Still, whatever the reason for not seeing him at Christmas, it was probably a very good one, she wasn't worried.

The radio was broadcasting the Kings speech to the nation, he spoke of the great sacrifice of those serving overseas and their families as well as the great sacrifice of those at home who had been victims of the bombing raids over the past months. But the message was also about hope, unity and peace at Christmas.

The words of King George VI reminded Rose of the soldier in the station. So many thoughts and questions still filled her mind, was he just delirious and had thought himself to be a soldier of the Great War, a blow to the head can cause dillusions and even hallucinations. There was also a more supernatural thought, that he really was a spirit. Whatever the answer, one thing she was sure of was that he was a good soul and there was no danger in him. She always felt a sense of sadness but also safety when she was around him. She also knew he didn't deserve to be alone on Christmas day. There was nothing left for her to do at home except listen to the radio, so she would take a walk to the station and make sure he was OK.

Although William had spent the vast majority of the day on his own, he had been at peace. For at least one day, there had been no pain, no thoughts of his past, no uncontrollable and unexpected grief. Just quietness and watching the Christmas joy of those who lived around Church Street Station. It had been a good day. The first good day for as long as he could remember.

There had been a few people on the station throughout the day, Mr Crispin had popped it to check on his kingdom, Sally had visited the tea shop for a few things she was missing at home and of course, the pub had opened over lunch. As he expected, everybody had ignored him as if he wasn't there. That troubled him a little.

All thoughts of being alone vanished as Rose greeted him for the second time that day.

"Good evening William".

"Rose, you should be at home, not coming to this cold station. It's very nice to see you though."

Rose made an excuse as if there was an alternative reason for her visit.

"Ah, well I had to check up on my flower cart, you never know who may be prowling around. I did also say that I'd pop in to see how you were before the day was out."

"Your flower cart has been safe all day. Nobody has been here causing trouble."

They both sat on the bench by platform one. Rose couldn't help but notice that William was strikingly handsome. He was quite boyish looking yet he had a very well trimmed mustache and deeply dark eyes. Despite his good looks, she couldn't help but notice that his skin seemed a little grey as if it was permanently cold. Again, she wondered about his family. Did he know if they were still around? She wondered why he wasn't trying to find them, especially at Christmas but then again, how could he. She dismissed the thought, if he wanted to talk about them then she would let him bring the subject up in his own time.

The casual conversation continued as the evening marched on with neither wanting to talk about anything that could cause awkwardness or upset. She still couldn't bring herself to telling him the truth.

As the tiredness of the day began to catch up with Rose, she got up to say goodbye to William for the evening. Tomorrow would see the end of the ceasefire and life would get back to normal including William's. She had enjoyed the more relaxed and untroubled persona and even had come to see him in a more friendly light.

"Are you going to be OK, William?" She was more concerned about the following day than the quiet night ahead.

He faced her and smiled "Don't worry about me, I'll deal with whatever comes, when it comes. You should get home, there are people here that need you more than I do." He was not just referring to her dad, he knew Jimmy had seen them. He knew Jimmy had strong feelings for Rose and couldn't interfere with that. He knew that he could not get involved with Rose in any way, let alone romantically. He had no idea how long he would be at the station or where he would go once he was no longer needed, He wasn't the same as Rose and Jimmy, he knew that. But his heart was reaching out to her. No matter how wrong it was, he couldn't help it.

As they stood facing each other, both had an overwhelming urge to kiss. For a moment, their faces moved closer together, it was wrong but something between them was overpowering. William suddenly stepped back. "You better go, Rose. It's getting late."

Rose's thoughts and hearts were racing but snapped back to reality as she realised what was happening. Embarrassingly, she apologised, turned and walked out of the station leaving William on his own once again.

As she walked back home, her mind was awash with confusion. She never meant for anything to happen between them. It couldn't happen, it was impossible. Besides she loved Jimmy. He was right for her, she knew Jimmy could take care of her and love her as she should be loved. He was real.

Christmas day 1940 was coming to an end on Church Street station. The spirit of peace had protected them all at least for one day and the horrors of the continuing war had no place in Great Britain on 25th December 1940. At least until tomorrow, all was calm.

CHAPTER NINE

BOXING DAY 1940

Christmas day had come and passed and the tenseness was beginning to show once again as the first faces appeared on this cold Boxing day morning. Expectations of a return to the bombings was on the forefront of everybody's mind in London. It was a case of 'when' and not 'if' the bombings would start again. Still, business needed to carry on as normal. Most couldn't afford the luxury of celebrating Boxing day as in times of peace. This was evident on Church Street station where the usual stalls and businesses were opening once more.

The tenseness in Church Street was not only due to the expected air raids but could also be felt around the newspaper stand as Jimmy began getting ready for the day. His usual cheeky, cockney ways were lacking as he went about getting ready to sell his fresh delivery of the Daily Herald, doing his best to ignore everybody around him.

He knew the day would prove awkward once Rose arrived. He wasn't angry with her, just upset that the feelings he had for her seemed one way. Since seeing her with that soldier last night his mind was playing out so many scenarios, none of which ended happily for him. But he kept telling himself that they were actually only chatting. Nothing else was going on. Somehow, he couldn't believe it was so innocent.

He was also concerned about the letter in his coat pocket. His time at Church Street was now short and despite what they both felt, he would have to tell her, and tell her today. His departure date to No:1 Initial Training Wing in Cambridge was 13th January. A little over a fortnight away. He wasn't troubled about where he was going as the brunt of attacks from the Luftwaffe has been in the South Eastern corner of England. Cambridge, although not near the coast and not exactly a high profile target still came under a certain amount of threat from air raids. Not that he feared for his own life but more for those who relied on him. His mother, siblings and of course, Rose. Despite the turmoil in his mind caused by the previous night, he loved Rose deeply and was terrified of seeing her hurt. Still, she needed to know.

Rose pulled her flower cart on to the station and set about getting ready for the post-Christmas trade. Her holly wreaths, mistletoe and other Christmas decorations were now missing and a new delivery of fresh plants and flowers adorned the cart. It was a shame they had to go, for a short while, they brought a welcome look of hope and cheer to a world surrounded by fear and destruction. Despite the passing of the festive season, trade would still be strong for her. In a time of war, that was a certainty.

As she finished setting up, she spotted Jimmy and walked across to him. "Morning Jimmy, surprised I didn't see you yesterday." She was smiling as she said it, there was no malice or bad feeling in the comment, just concern for him.

Jimmy had an urge to respond with his emotions but resisted. "Oh, you know how things are at home. The day came and went before I knew it. I did pop around to say hello but there was no answer. I guessed you had popped out for a while. How was your day?"

She could hear that he wasn't his normal self. Was something troubling him? "Oh, it was a quiet day. I popped out once or twice but was in most of the day. I must have just missed you. Jimmy, is something wrong?"

He wanted to talk about the soldier and why she was with him last night but again stopped himself from saying something he would regret later. I've got a little bad news I need to talk to you about. There's no easy way to say this. I'm going away for a while."

A wave of dread filled Rose. She had a strong feeling where this was going but she didn't want to admit it to herself. Jimmy would have to tell her. Her smile was replaced by a deep look of concern. "When? Where are you going?"

Jimmy reached into his coat pocket, pulled out the letter that he had received and hand it to her. She opened it and read the contents. As she read the letter, her eyes started to appear glassy until a tear emerged and rolled down her cheek. "You're leaving in just a few weeks? You can't go. You're needed here. So many people need you. Is there someone you can talk to?" She knew he had to go but didn't want to say goodbye to him.

"I have to go Rose, it's my duty. Besides Church Street station can always find a new paperboy."

Rose was now sobbing quietly. "I don't want you to go. I'll miss you terribly." She wrapped her arms around him and hugged him. She didn't want to let go as if he would stay as long as she held on.

Jimmy's heart softened and kissed her forehead gently. "It's OK, I'll be fine. You know what I'm like, I'm too lucky for anything bad to happen to me." He was desperately trying to reassure her. "Besides, they reckon this war will be over before the summer, I probably wont even leave England." He was lying, she knew that but she also knew he was doing his best to make her feel better. For that, she loved him.

"Please keep yourself safe Jimmy, I couldn't bear the thought of anything happening to you, it would break my heart." She pulled her head out of his chest and looked him in the eyes. "I love you Jimmy Deacon, don't ever forget that."

He was stunned. She had finally said it. All thoughts of the night before vanished as he leant forward and kissed her. The kiss seemed to last forever in his head. It was warm and made him feel very safe. He reassured himself that there was no longer anything to ask her about. Whatever happened last night was innocent. He would leave it at that.

Rose smiled at him softly. "I'd better get back to work, I've got a lot to catch up on and you've got lot's of newspapers to sell." He kissed her on the forehead again and they both turned and went back to their stalls.

As Rose returned she couldn't help thinking about the fleeting moment between William and herself the night before. She knew she loved Jimmy but she couldn't help the feelings for the mysterious soldier. She knew that it was a forbidden and impossible situation but still couldn't help the feeling nevertheless. Now, more than ever, Jimmy would need her. He would need her reassurance and her strength.

Jimmy felt the weight of the world lift off his shoulders. He was relieved that he had told Rose about being called up for service and her reaction had put to bed his fears about her feelings for the soldier. It was all in his head. He knew Rose was a kind and caring person and what he saw last night was nothing more than her caring. He still didn't understand what the soldier was doing at the station on Christmas day. He could just about understand that he had a job to do while trains were coming in and going out although he couldn't figure out what the hell that was but why did he spend Christmas day there? Maybe he should have a word with him and finally get some answers.

The 9:30am train to Portsmouth was being boarded and loaded, ready for the two hour trip to the coast. Amongst it's passengers were newly trained soldiers bound for service in Europe.

William looked on from his bench on Platform 1 at the wives kissing goodbye to their husbands. For some, it would be the last moments they spend together and he knew it. He didn't know how but he could see the wives who would return to the station that would need him and there was nothing he could do about it. He had tried to tell departing soldiers not to go but they all ignored him as if he wasn't even there. Was this a curse that he now had to live with? What could he have possibly done to deserve this? At least this train was not bringing pain to him. He was spared that, for now. But he knew before darkness fell he would be needed once again and the pain and torment would return.

He thought about his time with Rose the night before. It was her kindness that gave him strength to be able to deal with whatever was happening to him. But he had been getting too close to her. For a brief moment they had come close to kissing which he knew was so wrong. Despite the fact that he knew that she loved another, he was still unsure about how long he would be in this station. He wasn't even sure if he could love someone now. Of course, he knew he had the emotions to love but had no way of knowing what else he was capable of, at least until he had answers to why he was there.

The train whistled and slowly began to pull out of the station on its journey to Portsmouth. William wandered amongst the weeping wives, girlfriends and families waving goodbye to their loved ones. Again, he was completely ignored. That was understandable, he thought. They were all so engrossed with their farewell's, they naturally paid no attention to anything or anyone around them. Still, this was something which kept happening over and over again. In fact, as far as he knew, it was only Rose and the newspaper boy that had actually acknowledged he was there at all.

The train disappeared out of site and the last few relatives walked away. Amongst them were Dorothy Morgan, Sarah Mitchell, Mary James and Ruth Fitzpatrick. William knew their names. He didn't know how but knew he would soon see them again. He felt sadness for them, mostly because they were all unaware of what pain they would experience in the future. But he would be there for them, that, he was sure of.

Rose looked across at Platform 1 from her stall. As usual, William was sat on the bench by the platform and as usual he seemed far away with his thoughts. She had wanted to find the right moment to speak to him about what she knew about him. But the timing always seemed off, every time she tried, something would happen which would stop her. Even at this particular moment, she saw he was very distant again as if he was expecting something to happen again. She would leave him be for the time being.

She was snapped out of her train of thought by the loud announcement of the days headlines from Jimmy. Trust him to bring everything back to normal, she thought with a smile. She admired how cheerful he was being despite the knowledge that he would soon be leaving Church Street Station. She wondered how his mother, brother and sister were going to cope. He was the breadwinner of the family as well as taking on the role of the man of the house. They all depended on him but soon things would change. Of course, Jimmy wouldn't leave without making sure they were taken care of which included ensuring the majority of his RAF pay would get sent to his family each month. He would also cash in all of his 'stock' so, at least for a while, he knew they would be OK. Yes, Rose knew Jimmy would ensure everyone was taken care of. That was his way.

But it wasn't just his family that he would ensure was taken care of. For so long now, the whole of Church Street had come to rely on Jimmy for the little extra bargains that were otherwise unavailable. Rose wondered what they would do in the future once he'd gone. She also wondered how she was going to cope. She had grown very close to Jimmy and she loved him. Time would tell.

The 2:15pm train from Dover was bringing airmen back who had covered Christmas at the many airbases in the South Eastern corner of England. Mercifully for William, he was not needed on this particular train but he couldn't help but feel for the tired faces alighting. It was obvious that they were mentally and physically exhausted. Many had not seen their families for many months and were in desperate need of rest. At least for the next week they could enjoy time with their loved ones and bring in the new year together.

Although the unofficial two day lull in the bombings had come to an end, Boxing day had remained mostly quiet although the community was bracing itself for the return of the Luftwaffe. But at least for another night, relative peace was enjoyed.

CHAPTER TEN

THE REVALATION

Church Street station had been surprisingly quiet in the few days since Christmas. The raids had been very light and somewhat distant. The only tell tale signs were the far off thumps announcing that a few unprotected warehouses had been bombed on the outskirts of the capital by a pair of Stuka's chancing a surprise hit. Thankfully, there had been no casualties and damage had been relatively light. It was as if the attack wasn't intended to cause mass damage, rather test defences. Whatever the reason, the station was remaining quiet.

Since the peace of Christmas, there had been very few reasons for William's presence but he knew he couldn't leave. The unexpected quiet gave him the time to think back before the war, the Great War that is. Meeting Rose had reminded him of the girl he left back in Stafford. Jane Simmonds was just a year younger than William but stunningly beautiful. He could remember the shiny, fire-red hair that flowed right down her back and the beautiful blue eyes that would melt him every time he looked at her. She had a pale but innocent complexion and a naturally slender figure. She truly was beautiful. William had known Jane since they were at school but the young William had only seen her as someone he could pick on. It wasn't until they had both left school when he noticed the woman she was becoming. Over the next few years they would become good friends but William always wanted a little more. He could see himself settling down with her if only he could pluck up the courage to begin courting her. He was trying to build up the courage to ask her out on a date when the war began. He thought back to how his feelings for Jane were over-ridden by his sense of duty. But he intended to come home the hero and sweep her off her feet. But what now? Jane, his Mother and Father, his friends were all just memories. But memories of a life he wasn't part of anymore. He didn't know why or how, he just knew he would never go back or ever see them again. But that didn't stop him wondering what happened to them all. Did Jane find somebody else or did she keep herself for when he would come home? The very thought of it broke his heart. He would never have any way of knowing the truth. Maybe that's why he was getting so close to Rose. But Rose could never be like Jane. He couldn't fall in love again, not now. At least not until he could make sense of everything.

The morning of the 27th was just another normal day for Rose as she went about her business of setting up the flower stall for the days trade. Even though it had only been a few days since the festivities, it seemed like it was all over. That empty feeling that Christmas often leaves was showing all over the station even though they still had the New Year celebrations to come. Mr Crispin would leave the decorations up in the station until after the New Year as it still brought a festive cheer to the travellers. He was a traditionalist at heart and believed that all decorations should stay up until 6th January, the official end of the Christmas period. Sally Crispin however, was of the mind that she would return life to normal as soon as possible. Much to the annoyance of her father, she was already stripping the cafe of all evidence that it was ever Christmas.

For Rose, it was a normal day. Christmas had come and gone and that was it. An income had to be earned and the time for resting and celebrating was now over. Besides, it was only a matter of time before the air raid sirens would sound again and chaos would return. She never wanted to be a profiteer, taking advantage of the misfortunes of others but she did want to ensure that she could sustain both her father and herself should anything happen to the station. The war was making life so unpredictable, one never knew what the next day would bring.

One thing was sure though, she needed to speak to William. But how on earth was she going to bring the subject up. One doesn't just drop in that they think the other is dead and now a ghost. The very thought of it sounded insane, was she just over-thinking this and had let her imagination get away from her? Maybe there was another explanation to all of the mysteries surrounding the soldier. But what? How could she explain what she had witnessed? Why did he never leave the station area? There was also something else bothering her, since she had known him, she had not seen him eat, drink or sleep, Not once. There couldn't be any other answer, she thought. But the question still remained, how to tell him. It was pretty obvious to her that he seemed oblivious to it all or was in denial of the truth. She could see how that was possible. Maybe he just needed a friend to talk to about it. The one thing she was sure about was, it had to be today.

Since she had got to the station earlier, William had been sat on that same bench by Platform 1. Why that bench, by that platform? As she finished preparing the old wooden cart she looked across at him. He always seemed very deep in thought and unaware of what was going on around him while he sat on the bench. Now was the perfect moment. Jimmy had disappeared, the station was quiet and she would have William's full attention.

She walked across to the bench, dreading every step as she approached him. This was going to be difficult.

"Good morning William, what are you up to?"

William lifted his head to greet Rose "Morning Rose, not much, just thinking about a few things."

Rose seized the opportunity to ease into the conversation she needed to have with him. "I can understand that, I bet there are so many thoughts running around your mind at the moment. Is one of those thoughts, why you are here?"

"That question." He said the words as a statement. "The one thing that is continuously with me. How do you explain the impossible? It is too incredible to even think about, how did I time jump from 1916 to 1940 and what happened to all of my memories since. How did I get here on this station and why do I have this overwhelming compulsion to comfort people. I mean, I have no control over that, I just do it and then after I feel incredible pain. I mean real emptiness as though my heart has been ripped out. Yes, I think about these things quite a bit."

Rose swallowed hard. "William, I think I know what's happening to you. It seems impossible but I really can't see any other answer. I've seen things happening to you that can't be explained in any other way I'm just not sure how you're going to take it when I tell you what I think. It's been scaring me for a few days."

William looked at Rose, he could see she was having a hard time trying to tell him. "Why don't you just say it?" He said softly.

"OK." She paused briefly. "Before I say anything, what was the very last thing you can remember in 1916?"

He looked puzzled at the question. "Well, my last memories were being given the order to advance on to the German trenches. We all climbed up the ladders and then started to run forward. The noise was incredible, so loud. I can remember hearing so many bullets. It was like listening to wasps suddenly buzz by, but more violent. So many of the lads were dropping as they ran. So much blood. I can remember seeing the German trenches and the soldiers firing at us, I can remember getting closer, in fact so close I could see the face of one staring at me and then... Nothing. That's it. I can't remember anything else."

A chill ran down Rose's spine as she realised she was right. "William, I think you died on that battlefield. I don't know how but it makes sense. Well, it makes no sense at all but it seems like the only answer. I really think you are the spirit of William sent here to help others. I know it sounds crazy but..."

William cut her off mid sentence. "You think I'm a ghost? He started to laugh, more out of shock. "If I'm a ghost, then how can I be sat here talking to you?"

"The only people that see you is me and Jimmy. I've watched you when the trains come in. When you comfort people, they do not know you are there. They can't see, hear or feel you. I've seen it happen over and over again. I've also seen how you are once you have comforted them. You are overcome with grief, their grief. You take their pain away. You've said it yourself how you feel. I've also seen how at peace they are when they leave. That's why you are here."

William had gone quiet, he knew Rose was right but something was still fighting the logic of it. "I can't believe it Rose, if I died in France, then why can't I remember the moment. Surely it would have hurt. Surely I would have some memory of it. Maybe I was knocked silly and I have just got my memories back." He knew he was fighting the truth.

"Then tell me why you are still dressed in an outdated uniform? Soldiers don't dress like that anymore. Surely you've noticed that. You've seen the soldiers getting on and off the trains. You also do not appear to be a man of 46. You are just a young man William."

The truth was beginning to dawn on him. Rose was right, there was no other explanation. But why him? If he was dead, this is not what the bible said would happen. He didn't even believe in ghosts, when someone died they either went to Heaven or hell. That's what he had been taught at school and in church. If it was true, then why Rose and Jimmy. Why were they the only two that could see him? "What does Jimmy think?"

Rose smiled. "He doesn't know. He just thinks you're strange. It's probably a good idea that we don't tell him. It would only freak him out and cause more problems. I think as long as you leave him alone, he'll leave you alone. Besides he'll be gone soon."

"What do you mean 'gone'. Where's he going?"

"He's been called up for service in the army. He goes off to training in a couple of weeks."

The words filled him with dread. He didn't know why but he could feel pain. Rose saw it in his face.

"What's wrong William? You look worried."

"No, it's nothing. Just the thoughts of what we've been talking about." William had to lie to her. He felt that something was wrong about Jimmy leaving. Something dark but he didn't know what. He also didn't want to upset Rose, after all he wasn't sure himself.

"I know it must be a huge shock for you William, but I really do think something good is going to come from it all. There must be a reason why you were chosen. I think it's because you were a kind person. I think that whoever sent you here trusted you to be able to do the job."

Rose's words were comforting to him. If this was true, then it was possible Rose was the one person that could give him strength while he carried out the task he had been given. If this was true. It still seemed far-fetched. How does one accept that they are dead.

Rose noticed customers around her cart. "I have to go back to work but I'll only be over there if you need me." She got up to leave.

"Rose, please don't tell anybody about this. Especially Jimmy. He cannot know about me."

"Don't worry, I wont." She smiled. "Besides they'd all think I was barking mad."

She turned and walked back to her cart.

"What was that all about?" Jimmy questioned. He had got back to his stand in time to see Rose and William in deep conversation. "Is he still here? I mean what kind of geezer, soldier or not, wants to spend Christmas in a freezin' cold station. I must say, he seems to be taking a shine to you though." Jimmy teased.

"Jealous are we?" Rose taunted him. "No, just chatting. He's ok, he has his reasons why he's here but it's not any business of the likes of us. I just want to make sure he's ok, that's all. You know what I'm like." Rose was desperately trying to reassure Jimmy and divert the conversation away from the truth. She changed the subject quicklty.

"What does your mum say about you going away?

"Oh you know mum, she doesn't say a lot. She's worried but doesn't show it. I think it's a bit of a taboo subject in the house at the moment. The two kids don't seem to understand which is probably a good thing."

Rose put her hand on his arm reassuringly. "Don't worry, I'll keep an eye on them. Make sure they're ok."

"I know you will. I know everyone around here will be ok as long as you're around. You're the Angel of Church Street." He smiled.

"Oh, stop. I'm no such thing. We all look after each other here, that's the way it's always been and the way it always will be, no matter what."

Rose was right. The residents of Church Street were one big family who looked out for each other. Although Rose would look out for Jimmy's family, so would the other residents. No one was left wanting in the street. War torn London was certainly one of the times where people really needed each other. History would tell that the worst was still to come. London was about to be tested in ways not seen for centuries.

CHAPTER ELEVEN

LONDON'S BURNING...

Only God knows why man finds it necessary to inflict pain and death on his brother and sister. Land, money, love, greed, supremacy, all superficial reasons which always have an alternative way of reaching a solution. But despite all of the wars that have been fought throughout the ages and despite the countless millions of lives that have been lost, we still, even today, find it easier to kill rather than talk. This coming night, on the 29th December 1940 was to be one of those nights when the question of 'why' would be asked so many times.

For the inhabitants of Church Street, the morning of the 29th started quietly. A little too quiet maybe, still the nightly bombings had been all too sparse leaving a sense of uncertainty across London. A feeling that the city was being lulled into a false sense of security.

The station was eerily quiet in the few days after Christmas. Many of the local businesses would have to wait until after the New Year before normality would return, or at least as close to normality as the war would allow. Many wondered if 'normal' was a word that would need to be redefined as people grew accustomed to a new age of being in the violent path of Nazi Germany. So much had changed, yet the British people refused to bow down to a bully who would cowardly bomb them from afar. Yes, the British spirit, was definitely a tough nut to crack.

"I can't believe the left-whiffers 'aven't visited us recently" Sally said with a cigarette hanging out of her lips.

Rose chuckled "Luftwaffe, Sally" she said correcting the cafe owner.

"Yeah, whatever, but I sill think they're up to no good. Don't seem right at the moment, I've had a bad feelin' in me water for days now".

Rose couldn't help but laugh at the innocent ramblings of her friend, but she agreed with her. There was something not quite right in the air. The current climate seemed like the definition of 'a false sense of security'. Little did they all know they would only have to wait a few hours to be proved right.

Rose and Sally weren't the only one's feeling the unsure pressure. William had an extreme sense of anxiety about him. Something was wrong, very wrong. The air around him was heavy with a sense of dread. He couldn't explain it but he knew something very bad was on it's way, something far worse than anything he knew. He didn't know what but he knew it was coming and coming soon.

He sat on the bench by Platform one next to a man reading a newspaper. Of course, the man had no idea that the adjoining seat was now occupied by the soldier but an icy shiver suddenly engulfed him making him stand and look around for the source of the chill. It was if he had suddenly been wrapped in a blanket of Arctic air, yet he seemed to be the only one reacting to it. Bewildered, he walked away looking for signs that others may have felt it too.

William knew only too well why the stranger suddenly felt cold, yet he was still having a hard time accepting the reality of his situation. Maybe there was another reason? Damn, it only he could make sense of it all. But the fact remained that the man he sat next to, although unaware, felt his presence. William knew the man couldn't see him yet still didn't know why.

He spotted Rose at her cart going about her normal daily routine of arranging her flowers and getting ready for the day's trade. He got up and wandered over to her. As he walked over towards her, he couldn't help but feel a sense of danger towards her. Yet again, he didn't understand why but something was very wrong and she was in danger. As he got close to her, she turned as if she knew he was approaching. As she turned to face him, she pulled her shawl around her tightly as if to protect herself from a sudden draft. She could see the worry on his face.

"Good morning William, is there something wrong? You look worried."

"I don't know Rose, something feels wrong. Everything is quiet and peaceful but I'm getting a sense of something very bad. I can't help but feel that you're all in danger. You need to leave London." William didn't know why he was saying this to Rose, he just knew that he had to warn her, but of what? He must have seemed, at the very least, irrational and panicky to her.

"What do you mean William, there's nothing happening at the moment, everything seems OK"

"I know, but... I don't know what, I just feel that something isn't right. Please Rose, Get your dad and Jimmy away from here for a while."

For the first time Rose was beginning to feel uncomfortable around the soldier, she didn't want to be scared by him and he was scaring her now.

"William, I don't know what's going on with you but we're perfectly safe here. Besides, I can't just pick up and leave. I need to work or we don't eat. I'm sure everything is just fine."

William knew that he couldn't get his warning across to her, but his failure only heightened his anxiety.

"Just be careful today, promise me."

"Nothing is going to happen, William, I'm fine. We're all fine, you've got nothing to worry about. Now, you need to excuse me, I've got a lot of work to do". Rose cut him off and went back to working on her cart.

William walked away from Rose, he felt he had crossed a line with her and pushing her any further wouldn't help matters. He looked across to Jimmy, who was crying out the day's newspaper headlines to passers-by in a hope to sell his daily quota. Maybe, he would have better luck convincing Jimmy to persuade Rose to go. After all, he would do anything to protect her.

"Jimmy, I need to talk to you." The newspaper vendor ignored him and continued his patter. "Jimmy, we need to talk." He said louder. Still, Jimmy seemed to ignore him. "Jimmy! Look at me." Still nothing. A sense of dread suddenly filled his mind, Jimmy couldn't see or hear him. What was happening? He ran back over to the Flower stall.

"Rose, something's wrong, Jimmy can't see me."

Rose shivered and looked around and then turned back to her cart and continued working.

"Rose." Nothing "Rose." He was on his own. Something had changed. He was alone. Rose wouldn't just ignore him, he really was a spirit. The cold, hard reality hit him like a bomb blast. He wandered back over to the bench and sat down, alone and very scared. He felt powerless. Powerless to warn the woman that he'd grown so fond of, powerless to warn anybody of what he was feeling. It was if someone was not allowing him to warn them of impending danger. Maybe he couldn't interfere with the natural order of events, no matter how deadly or tragic the outcome.

It was 6:00pm and the night time had once again shadowed the capital. William had sat on the bench all day worrying about the bad feeling that had been with him. He was also feeling a massive sense of loneliness since realising that Rose could no longer see him. Mercifully, the days trains had been kind to him, the lull in hostilities had also meant that the pain of wives and families of those lost had also been absent for the past few days. But as the night took a grip, his apprehension only grew stronger into a sense of inevitable dread.

Despite the early darkness, trains continued to depart and arrive at Church Street giving the station businesses extra opportunity to get a few final customers before 'Blackout' rules came into force. Of course, Rose and Jimmy made the most of the extra trade. After all, a few extra pennies could make all the difference in the current climate. But Jimmy and Rose finally called it a day and began their routine of packing away their businesses.

"That's it for me Rose, my trade has dried up for the day, can't get blood out of a stone, as they say."

Rose smiled. "I know how you feel, it seems nobody has the money for flowers since Christ..."

Rose was cut off mid sentence as the air raid sirens began to howl.

"Here we go again, I was wondering when ol' Adolf was gonna get bored and send his planes back." Jimmy seemed almost nonchalant as the faint drone of bombers aprroached, gradually getting louder as the seconds passed.

"We better get below before it all starts. We don't want to be up here if the station gets hit again." Rose was remembering the last time the bombs fell.

As they got into the old underground station, the drone of the planes over head echoed powerfully in the tunnel but there were no explosions from falling bombs. Just the sound of lots of metal clattering on the ground.

"That's wierd, I was expecting all hell to break loose. Where's all the bangs?" Jimmy was feeling uneasy. He certainly dreaded the explosions but this was worse. "Stay down here Rose, I'm going to see what's going on."

"No Jimmy, wait until we get the all clear. We don't know what's up there."

"Just wait here, I'll just be a minute."

"Jimmy, no..." But he was already heading back up the stairs. As he reached the main station, he saw bright lights glowing through the windows but the glows were not from the street lamps. The strong light was accompanied by an eerie hiss which sent a chill through his bones. He ran over to the entrance to the station and looked out down Church Street. Fires were burning in almost every building and the streets were littered with small burning cylinders. Jimmy looked out beyond Church Street and could see the same glow all over the city. London was literally burning down.

Firemen and volunteers were rushing around Church Street with buckets of water and sand doing what they could to keep the blazes under control but this battle was being lost very quickly as the flames from the burning buildings reached higher in to the London night sky.

One of the incendiary's had landed by a service entrance to the station and had ignited the wooden door. Jimmy ran towards the fire removing his jacket to beat out the flames as he ran. He kicked the burning cylinder in to the street to burn out harmlessly and then attcked the flames with his jacket. He shouted out for help but those who where still in the street were too busy fighting other fires. The door frames and surrounding timbers were also alight, he had to stop it before the flames reachd the roof beams. If they caught the station would be doomed. Slowly the flames reduced until Jimmy finally stamped out the last dying glows.

He ran into the station and grabbed one of the fire buckets that had been placed around the station, he ran back to the black, smoking door and threw the water over it to stop the flames reigniting. In all of the commotion, he had become unaware of the smoke he was inhaling which was now making him cough uncontrollably. He stumbled away from the smoke gasping for air and gagging on the thick smoke burning his lungs. He took a few slow breaths of clean air and began to calm down. He wiped his streaming eyes, stood up and walked back inside towards the underground station.

Across the city, fires were raging out of control as the first wave of the air attack passed leaving thousands of incedaries in its wake. There were too many fires for the Fire Brigade to handle and the heart of London glowed out of control. But there was more to come...

William was watching on helplessly. He was sat on his bench by Platform 1 with his mind screaming in pain as he felt the horror of thousands of souls. He felt an unbelievable urge to reach out to help all that were suffering on this night but he couldn't. He simply couldn't reach them. The pain was burning through his mind as if one of the firebombs was inside his head. He had seen Jimmy fighting the fire but couldn't help. Still the question raged within him of why he could no longer be seen by Rose and Jimmy. What had he done to deserve all of this? His thoughts were interrupted by the air raid sirens sounding once more.

"Not again." muttered a tired Jimmy, still trying to clear his lungs of smoke. The air raid sirens echoed with a droning base note through the underground tunnels causing its occupants to block their ears from the noise.

"Jimmy, don't go up again." Rose could see the tiredness and pain in his face and was worried for her young friend. Jimmy said nothing, he simply stared at the ground listening out for whatever was about to fall from the skies.

The low hum of the planes could be heard down in the underground station long before they were above the city, so could the explosions as the bombs fell to commence the second phase of the raid. As the planes got closer, it was as if the volume was being raised on the explosions until all hell broke loose.

A massive explosion, and then another, and another. Church Street was finally taking direct hits. The lights in the underground suddenly went out and masses of dust consumed the platform. The lights flickered and then came back on causing a dusty fog which filled the eyes and throats of those taking shelter. For a moment there was nothing but silence and then more explosions, but further away.

"Stay down!" Jimmy shouted and then ran back up the stairs to the main station. The station was a mass of rubble and broken glass. A bomb had hit just by the station entrance destroying it as well as the station pub. He looked up at the roof, not a pane of glass was intact. Looking up to the open skies, he could see the streams of tracer from the anti-aircraft guns, fruitlessly searching for the Luftwaffe. Dozens of small fires were burning around the remains of the station entrance. Yet again, he feared for the reamaining station structure. He ran back down the stairs to the underground.

"I need the men to come up and help put these fires out!" he shouted out.

A dozen men got up and headed toward the stairs where Jimmy directed them to help put out the fires in the station.

Rose could no longer stay down in the tunnels, she ran up the stairs and was met with the devastation.

"What the hell is going on?" she screamed at Jimmy as she reached the entrance.

"I don't know Rose, I really don't know."

Just then Rose felt a chill run over her body as she remembered.

"DAD!" She sprinted up Church Street to her house and stopped with ther mouth open as she stared at the pile of rubble where she used to live. She screamed and then clawed at the bricks and mortar fearing the worst, crying and calling for her Dad as she dug. Jimmy was close behind her and knew that there was no hope. The house had taken a direct hit and was destroyed instantly. Her father who had been sleeping on the ground floor bedroom, mercifully, never knew what happened.

Jimmy grabbed Rose and pulled her away from the wreckage. She was crying wildly and struggling to get back to digging for her father.

"Rosie, come on, let me take you back to the station, there's nothing you can do here". The ARP wardens were telling everybody to stay away as there was a strong smell of gas. With all of the burning debris strewn around, there was a big risk of a massive problem. Still, Rose couldn't leave, she needed to get to her father, no matter what. Jimmy had to forceably move her back to the station.

Despite the damage to the entrance, the pub and all of the windows, the station was mostly still in tact. Of course it would take a good while to clean up and carry out sufficient repairs for it to get back to service but the old building still stood. However, Church Street had take three direct hits from the air raid, including the bomb that had hit Rose's house, the street was devastated.

But despite these tragic events, the danger had far from passed. Fires were still raging from the incediary bombs. To make matters worse, a wind had began to fan the flames which only aided the fires to spread to ajoining buildings. The thousands of fires around the city had completely overwhelmed the fire brigade who were now facing dwindling water supplies. The air raid had been planned to take place during low tide on the Thames causing the hoses to clog with mud or even worse, the water becoming unreachable. London had not seen anything like this since the Great Fire of London in 1666.

Despite the continuous bombings, the burning buildings and the ever-growing firestorm, the residents of Church Street were out doing their best to help put out the fires, tend to the injured, pull people out of the rubble or simply do whatever they could. That was the way of the people of London. Determined, unwaivering, resilliant, and stubborn in the face of an enemy which was determined to break the spirit of the British people. Buildings may have been burning but so was the passion in the hearts of the Londoners to stand up to foreign bullies.

During that night, 160 people lost their lives in the raid and 250 were injured. The bombing was over by 9:45pm but the firestorm would rage on until 4:00am. Hitler had targeted St Paul's Cathedral, hoping such a loss would break the British spirit sufficiently for an invasion to take place. Despite being hit by the incediary bombs, St Paul's remained standing, although it had suffered some damage but thanks to the bravery of the fire marshalls, this remained fairly minor. The invasion never came.

It had just passed 10:00pm at Church Street station and Rose was sat sobbing to herself on one of the few station benches that were still intact. Although she had been over-whelmed with grief, she was feeling an unexpected calmness flow over her. Dad was gone. Volunteers on Church Street had managed to dig out his body and it had been taken away to the rapidly filling hospital morgue.

Rose was glad that he had been found. She wouldn't have been able to bear the thought of him lying under all of that rubble on his own. She felt a little comfort knowing that at least she could say goodbye to him properly. She didn't feel any anger or extreme emotion at those who had carried out the attack, she wasn't losing control like she felt she should, she just felt peace. She couldn't understand why even to the point that she felt a little guilty. But she was at peace.

Unbeknown to Rose, William stood directly behind her, his hand on her shoulder feeling her pain drain into his heart. The tears streamed down his face, not from taking her pain but the knowledge that the one person he could trust in this mad world had her heart broken. He so wanted to comfort her with his words but still, she could not see or hear him. All he could do was help her the way he helped everyone else, but it wasn't enough. He wanted to do more. He stayed with her until Jimmy showed up to take her away from the horrors of Church Street and then watched her walk away, Jimmy's arm wrapped tightly around her shoulders. He so wanted to be in Jimmy's place.

As he resigned himself to the fact that Rose no longer needed him that night, he knew his work was far from over. He would be needed by so many that night. In more ways than one, tonight would experience The Spirit of Christmas 1940 in more ways than one.

CHAPTER TWELVE

AFTERMATH...

An acrid, dense mixture of smoke, sulphur and morning moisture filled the air as dawn broke on Church Street. The local people wore exhausted expressions on their faces as they continued to douse the remaining flames and embers and continue the search for survivors still trapped in the tons of rubble and the grim task of digging out the bodies of those poor souls who were tragically lost in the attack. The search would go on for days to come, bringing the inhabitants to the very brink of despair but their spirits would remain in tact. Despite the vicious and tragic events, the British people refused to be bullied and beaten.

James Crispin stood staring at what remained of the station entrance. He felt an immense sense of anger but yet determination to find a way to get his station back to business. So much tragedy had affected his small empire, how would things ever be the same again? It wasn't the damaged entranceway or the skylight glass splintered across the floor, everything could be swept up and rebuilt, even the pub that had taken much of the blast could be repaired. It was his family, the people who kept the station running on a daily basis, they were the ones who were damaged the most. He wandered over towards the Swan, the station pub. There was a huge hole in the front wall which gave way to the damage inside. Everything inside had been destroyed, the furniture, the bar itself, every piece of glass. But the more he looked at it the more he thanked God. His brother Stan and his wife Esther were safely in the underground along with his James's daughter, Sally. Sally's Cafe lost it's front window but was more or less intact apart from the brick dust and broken glass. Yes, in a few days he would be able to clean up and repair enough to start a temporary service while other, more major repairs were carried out. The station was damaged but not destroyed. It would live on. His thoughts turned to his treasured flower seller, Rosie. She would need so much support and help. In one moment, she had lost so much. Her father was her reason for her way of life. She never saw it as a chore, it was her dad, he had given her so much over the years and she loved looking after her hero dad in his later years. James vowed to himself to help her in every way he could.

William had witnessed it all, he had seen the devastation over the street and felt the pain of those who suffered but none was more painful than that of his friend. Despite all of his abilities to take pain from the suffering, he wished that he could have done more to help her. This was not a gift, it was a curse. A curse to wander this station mopping up the damage that this war left behind. What could he have possibly done in his former life to deserve this.

His train of thought was interrupted by a voice behind him.

"I should have known you'd show up now it's all over. Come to gloat over all of us, have you?" It was Jimmy, he could see William once more. William stumbled back in shock as the realisation washed over him. "Where's Rose? I need to see her."

"You stay away from her, the last thing she needs is the likes of you upsetting her even more."

"I just need to..."

Jimmy stopped him mid sentence. "Don't you dare. Keep away from her, I'm warning you."

He walked away, his fists were clenched in anger even though he knew all of this wasn't the soldiers fault. He was covered in dirt, ash and cuts and bruises. His clothes were ripped and filthy but he didn't care. He had taken Rose to his house, his mother would look after her, she knew how to. Seeing Rose in so much pain was just too much for him to take, he didn't know what to do or say to her, the best thing was to just let mum do her thing. Yes, that was best. He didn't want to say the wrong thing to her and upset her further. What was he thinking? He knew he was just avoiding her because he didn't know how to be around her. Maybe taking a little time would help. He would pop back in a while and see her. But he needed to see the station and make sure everyone was OK. He also needed to see just how damaged the station was. A lot of people depended on the station, not just for traveling but for livelihoods. But he knew everyone would chip in, him included.

Midday came and still the clean up continued. Nobody had slept but despite their exhaustion, they continued and would stay until the job was done. And there was so much to be done.

Sally had cleaned the cafe as best she could and was keeping everybody going with cups of tea and sandwiches. At least, this was one part of the station that could still operate. It had taken her just a couple of hours to clean the cafe to a standard where she could operate, one of the station staff had cleared out the rest of the glass from the window frame and had put a board in its place so at least she could secure it temporarily. She had just taken a cup of tea out to her dad when she glanced across to the entrance of the station. She saw a figure standing amongst the rubble looking in. She was bedraggled and filthy, her hair was matted and messy and her face was caked in filth. "Oh my God, it's Rosie".

She ran over and embraced her, Rosie didn't move. Her face was expressionless and staring into nowhere, it was as if she didn't even realise Sally was there. Sally guided her over to the cafe and sat her down just outside at a table she had set out for the workers. Still, Rosie was just staring into nothingness. Her beautiful smile and innocent looks were gone. All that was left was an empty shell. Her emotions had been so intense that they had finally blocked her thoughts.

Sally sat with her and held her hand. "I'm so sorry Rosie, is there anything I can do?"

Rose wasn't listening, she continued to stare when a tear emerged from her eye and rolled down her face.

"There's nothing left, it's all gone. Dad, my home, everything's gone." It was obvious shock had taken over and was now controlling her. She slowly turned to Sally. "I don't know what to do, I don't know what to do next, Sally. What do I do?"

"Oh sweetheart, it'll be OK, we'll all help you, I promise. You won't be alone." Sally was trying to be positive but she knew nothing could take her pain away. "Jimmy said you can stay with his family as long as you like and you know my door is always open. I have a spare room that you are welcome to if you need a little peace and quiet."

Suddenly, her empty look changed to a sinister and angry glare. Without saying another word and ignoring everything else around her, she got up and walked towards Platform 1. She had spotted William. He got up off the bench as he saw her walking towards him.

"Rosie, I..."

"WHERE WERE YOU? WHY DIDN'T YOU DO ANYTHING? I NEEDED YOU LAST NIGHT AND YOU WEREN'T HERE. WHY WASN'T I GOOD ENOUGH TO BE HELPED? AS SOON AS YOU THOUGHT THERE WAS TROUBLE YOU DISAPPEARED ON US. YOU'RE A COWARD! WHY DON'T YOU BUGGER OFF TO WHERE YOU CAME FROM AND LEAVE US ALONE!"

She started crying uncontrollably and dropped to her knees.

"Just leave us alone William, Just go." He put his hand on her shoulder hoping to help her.

"DON'T TOUCH ME, LEAVE ME ALONE." she screamed.

He let go and stood back, frightened by her reaction. He knew he couldn't tell her he was with her throughout it all, he knew she wouldn't believe him. He walked away, he needed to give her time. She needed to get over the initial shock of what had happened to her before he could talk to her. He walked out of the station, he was aware of the hatred stares of Jimmy as he left.

"Hey Rosie, you OK?" Jimmy had seen what had happened and couldn't just sit back and do nothing.

"Hello Jimmy, I don't know. I don't know what to feel. All I know is I'm now alone, I've got nothing left, I want my dad back."

"I know, sweetheart. I know you're hurting so much at the moment but you will be OK, you're strong and wonderful and you will get to the other side of this. But you are not alone, you will never be alone."

She wrapped her arms around him and sobbed. "Please don't leave me Jimmy, promise me you'll help me".

"I'm not going anywhere, you got me for keeps." He pulled her in closer to him and kissed the top of her head but also thinking to himself that he had just made a promise he couldn't keep. He was leaving in the near future to join up and there was nothing he could do about it. But Rosie didn't need to hear that or be reminded of it. She was well aware of what was going to happen but she needed comfort right now, not more things to worry about.

So, the most devastating attack on London ever had taken place but the plan to bring Great Britain to its knees had failed. Despite the devastation, London was already starting to recover. It simply just wouldn't be beaten. For Rose, the coming days would prove difficult as she came to terms with the loss of her father and losing her home. But the funeral would bring a chance to say goodbye to him properly and lay him to rest with dignity. She would continue to mourn him but the tears would slowly be replaced with cherished memories.

Church Street Station was closed for a whole two days before the trains began running again and normality began its road to recovery. Temporary repairs had been made to the entrance so that it was safe enough for the public to use. The pub had been closed off with barriers while it was being repaired and the roof glass was already being replaced.

James Crispen walked out of the entrance of the station, looked up to the skies, stuck two fingers up to where the bombs had recently come from and shouted out "SOD OFF HITLER, WE'RE STILL STANDING!" He then went back in to the station to commence business once again.

CHAPTER THIRTEEN

THE WEAKENING...

It was 11th January, a Saturday and it had been almost a fortnight since the big attack on London and Church Street station was close to fully operational once more. The entrance had been repaired enough for normal daily use although the new bricks told a story of the damage incurred from the bombing. The glass had been replaced in the roof and Sally's cafe had a new front window. The pub was slowly being repaired but it wasn't essential for the day to day running of the station and therefore remained closed and barricaded off to the public. But, the pub aside, it was business as usual once more. It seemed like Christmas was nothing more than a distant memory and the New Year had been overshadowed by the attack. The festive spirit had come to an end on that night prematurely and very cruelly.

Mercifully, there had been no more raids on Church Street which gave its inhabitants precious time to recover as best they could although the air raid warnings remained constant as bombs continued to fall in other parts of the city.

William still found himself on the station platform each morning although he kept out of the way of Rose who had now returned to her flower stall. He was very wary of causing here anymore distress although he wanted so much to speak to her. He needed to let her know the truth about that awful night but maybe she really didn't want him around anymore. Besides, Jimmy had been constantly watching him ensuring he kept his distance. Over the last few days Jimmy had been on the station less and less, despite this, William decided to keep to himself. The fact that Jimmy was watching him and the fact that he was avoiding Rose caused more concern for him. Why could they not see him on that day yet they could now? What was causing the changes? Why was this happening?

But the trains were now coming in as normal and he was still needed but the night of the 29th had taken its toll on him and he no longer wanted this responsibility. He wanted it to finally end but he didn't know how that was possible. All he could do was hope that all of this would be over soon.

Since that dreadful night he had felt weaker and was finding it harder and harder to comfort those poor souls on Platform 1. It was as if every person he comforted took something out of him that couldn't be replaced. He was beginning to fade slowly. A train was due in to the platform soon and he was filled with fear. Fear that he had to comfort more heartbroken people, fear that he was losing his strength and maybe soon, he would be no use, just doomed to witness the pain of loss at its very worst. The thought of this was unbearable. Although he wanted this, whatever it was, to be over, he had a lot of things to make right while he still could.

Rose was back at her flower cart after the hardest moments of her life. Although her fathers funeral had given her some closure, she was still broken. She had returned to work two days previous and was struggling. So much had changed in her life and was also about to change. In two days time Jimmy was off to begin his basic training and would be away for some time. Ever since the bombing her mind had been taken up by the sad duties she needed to perform and salvaging the very few items of property that had survived the bomb blast so Jimmy's departure was not in the forefront of her mind. But now she was back on the station, she could think of nothing else.

Of her house, very little had survived. Of course, there would be compensation for the building under advance payments for post-war damage but she knew very well it would take months, even years and a mountain of paperwork and red tape to cut through before she would see a penny. But she had been welcomed and supported at Jimmy's house by his whole family and, at least for the time being, this was now home. But she wouldn't stay there for free, so it was back to the flower cart to earn her keep. At least by paying rent and helping out with the house chores, she could feel a little better about her practical situation.

Since returning, she had been aware that William was back to Platform 1. She felt guilty about her outburst at him, she knew that nothing had been his fault and there must have been a very good reason for him not to be on the station during the bombing. But she had hurt him deeply with what she said and somehow couldn't bring herself to talk to him. Maybe once Jimmy had gone, she could talk to him. She was very aware of Jimmy's feelings towards William and didn't want to cause a problem between the two. She would wait until things were a little less complicated. Her train of thought was interrupted by the young cockney.

"Good morning gorgeous, how're you feeling today?"

"Hello Jimmy, I'm OK, just a little tired."

"You don't have to be here, you know. You can go home and rest."

"I know, but you'll be leaving in a few days and you're mum is going to need every penny coming in to the house. I need to do my bit. Besides, working helps me to keep my mind off what happened, the less I think about it, the better."

"Hey, you need to stop worrying about the money thing, I've left plenty to tide you all over for a while but I understand why you want to work. Just don't burn yourself out."

"Oh Jimmy, you're sweet for caring. Thank you." She kissed him lightly on the lips and a small smile appeared on her face. It was the first smile for a long time. Then just like that it was gone again. Jimmy left her to her thoughts and her work. She would be OK, it would just take time. As he walked across the station he eyed William. Still, his contempt for him was strong, he wasn't sure why, he just knew he wasn't good for Rose, especially at the moment. He was worried that he would get back inside her head once he left and that was a problem. He would need to do something to stop that and soon.

The 11:15 train arrived at Platform 1 from Portsmouth, this was the train William had been dreading. Families and friends of loved ones as well as the outgoing passengers were gathered ready for when the train came to a stop and the doors were opened. William had been watching one family. He knew this family would need him in the next few minutes.

The train slowly emptied its passengers and then refilled with new ones leaving just a few remaining people waiting hopelessly including the family that William had been watching. A uniformed man stepped off the train and approached the family and spent a few minutes talking to them. The elder woman, the missing soldiers mother suddenly dropped to her knees and cried out as the sad news was delivered. David Boyle was only 19, just a boy. He had only been in the RAF a year being drafted straight from basic training to Europe. He had been a Bombers gunner during the raid on Bremen and had been shot down and killed, along with the rest of his crew on the return.

By instinct, William walked over unnoticed by all, apart from Rose, to the woman and knelt beside her. He placed his hand on her shoulder and was instantly overcome by what he felt was flames inside his head. The burning feeling spread throughout his body as if he was inside the burning airplane as it descended to its doom. He fell to the side of the woman and was writhing in agony on the ground, he couldn't stand this pain, it had never been so intense before. He screamed out loud in pain, unheard and unseen by everyone around him. The family helped the mother to her feet and they slowly left the platform leaving William on the ground where he fell.

Rose could stand it no longer, she ran over to platform 1 and knelt down beside William. She put her hand on his cheek, he was burning up. Before he had been icy cold but now his skin was physically too hot to touch.

"William, what's going on, what can I do?" William rolled slowly over to look at her.

"Don't touch me Rose, I don't know what's happening."

"Let's get you up on to the bench". She helped him up to his feet, his uniform was also hot from his body. He stumbled across to the bench and slumped down.

It's OK Rose, just leave me here, I'll be OK. I just need a little time."

"OK, but I'll be over at my cart if you need me." He didn't reply, he simply waved her away. She left but looked back as she walked. The anger that she felt towards him after the attack had gone and was replaced by concern for him. Yet again, he had given himself for someone else. There was nothing bad or evil about this man. Whoever or whatever he was, he was not here to cause pain but relieve it. She thought back to that night, she remembered an unexplained sense of calm in the most terrible time. Then it hit her, he had been with her, she couldn't see or hear him but he had been there all along. She was starting to see him for what he really was, he was an angel. A very strange angel but one nonetheless. But something was different, when he helped people before, he recovered fairly quickly but as she looked back she could see that he was suffering worse than he ever had.

She watched him as he got up slowly and stumbled across the station towards the entrance as if he had just been injured. His face looked ashen and aged, "My God," she thought. "What was happening to him?"

Jimmy was beside her once more looking as shocked as she was.

"I can't believe what I have just seen. Rose, did that really happen?" he asked as William finally got to the station entrance and disappeared from view. Jimmy had seen everything.

"Yes Jimmy, that really happened. I don't know how or why but what you saw was very real."

"That woman was inconsolable and it was if he took all of her pain on to himself. Who the hell is he?"

"Language Jimmy," she snapped. All of a sudden the old Rose was back. "Honestly, I don't know who or what he is but I do know he doesn't mean us any harm."

"All of this time I thought he was some kind of weirdo just hanging around. But he's not, is he?"

"No, he's not. But I also think he's getting weaker and weaker. He needs help before he..." She didn't know how to finish that sentence.

"Before what, Rose?"

Would he just fade away? How can an angel die, if he really was an angel.

"I don't know Jimmy, I really don't know."

So much had changed in one single day. Devastation had been subsided, hatred had been defeated and pain had been mercifully lifted all because of one soul. Mysteriously, only two witnessed the truth. But in this case, the truth could not be logically explained. Rose and Jimmy vowed to keep this to themselves as firstly, no one would believe them anyway and secondly, this was something that shouldn't be public knowledge. To them, William was a blessing to Church Street station and all those who travelled to or from it. To William, he was living a curse which he didn't understand. The questions that he had for the past few weeks remained unanswered for the time being.

CHAPTER FOURTEEN

SAYING GOODBYE...

The day had come that Jimmy and Rose had dreaded. Jimmy's train to Cambridge was leaving at 10:00am and they both wanted to make the most of the time left. After Jimmy said goodbye to his family, they left the house early and walked to the station together arm in arm. There had been precious little time for feelings between them over the past fortnight but the inevitablity of the day brought them together for a final few hours.

Jimmy was dresssed in his best suit, he was determined to make a good impression. If he was joining the RAF, he was going to make the most of it and get himself into aircrew. He knew he wasn't clever enough to become a pilot or navigator but there were plenty of positions as gunners or a bomb aimer. Failing that, he could consider air defence of the air fields. All of these jobs would carry an eliment of risk but if he was going to go into battle, he wanted it to be on his terms.

Rose did think he looked very hansome in his suit though, she was used to seeing him in his old coat, a jumper and his work trousers. She wondered how nice he would look in his new uniform. Although she feared for him, she was looking forward to that.

"You will look after yourself, won't you Jimmy. And you will write to me as much as you can?" She asked.

"Rosie, there's no need to worry, I'll be fine. And of course, I will write. Mum packed a writing pad and plenty of envelopes for me to use. Not sure how good the post is though. Mind you they may post me close to home after training and I might be able to pop home every now and then or you could visit."

This made Rose feel a little easier, she was dreading the thought of him being posted overseas and not seeing him for a long time.

"Oh I do hope so. It'd be so lovely to be close to you, or at least within reach by a train journey."

"Let's see what happens once my training is done. If I manage to get into aircrew, I'll be in England for some time. We may even get the chance to get get married if you like."

Rose stopped in her tracks, he had just proposed completely out of the blue and it caught her off guard.

"Jimmy, are you asking me to marry you?"

"Um, yes." He looked sheepish as if he had just crossed a line.

"Oh Jimmy, yes. Oh, yes, I'd love to marry you. Oh you don't know how much this means to me." She was smiling as she looked at him, letting the thought of being his wife wash over her. He kissed her tenderly.

"I love you Rosie, more than you know."

"Oh Jimmy, I love you too."

They continued their walk to the station, talking as they went. Rose was now clutching his arm tightly with her head resting on his shoulder. She felt safe and happy once again. Something which was unexpected. During the past few weeks, she had very little reason to smile nor did she want to but Jimmy had been her strength to get through her hardest times. But now, she wanted to scream out from the highest buildings with hapiness.

As they entered the station, Jimmy was met by his other family, the station workers. James Crispin was the first to approach him.

"Good luck Jimmy, we're all very proud of you. Just make sure you come back home and see us soon, this old station won't be the same without your voice screaming out the headlines."

"I will Mr Crispin, I promise."

Sally was next to wish him well. She gave him a big hug and kissed him on the cheek.

"Don't worry, we'll look after her." she said looking towards Rose. He smiled at Sally.

"Thank you, Sal."

For the next few minutes, the regular staff each took their turn at wishing Jimmy well until once again, he was alone with Rose. They headed over towards Platform 1, where his train was due in shortly. As they walked, Jimmy spotted William sat on his bench.

He turned to Rose.

"Rosie, give me a moment." He released he arm and walked over to the soldier.

"Look, I don't know you or I don't pretend to know why you're here but I was wrong about you. I saw what happened the other day and, although I don't understand what happened and to be honest I don't want to know, I do know you're OK. Just do me a favour and keep an eye on these people for me."

William stood up, though he seemed unsteady on his feet. "I'll do my best. You, please stay safe." He put his hand out towards Jimmy. Jimmy shook his hand which felt like an ice block. He was taken back at how cold William was. He smiled and walked back over to Rose.

Rose was moved by what she had just seen. She never thought, in a month of Sundays that they would have parted in a friendly way.

"Jimmy, that was so beautiful." she said to him as he arrived back by her side. He smiled at her and they turned and walked on to the platform to wait for the train.

William's heart sank when he saw the couple walk on to the station arm in arm. He had a soft spot for Rose and although he knew that nothing could ever happen between them, he still felt that she was getting further and further away from him. Things had been turbulent for a while but he thought she still cared for him, especially after the concern she showed him two days ago. But even if there was no Jimmy a relationship between them would be quite impossible. She was a local girl who belonged to this town and to this station and he was... well, he was still not sure where he belonged or how long he would be here for. In fact, there were still so many unanswered questions. No, he couldn't allow himself to be involved with anyone in anyway.

Rose aside, he was worried. When he shook Jimmy's hand he felt a sense that he couldn't explain. He couldn't be sure if it was good or bad but he definitely felt something. All he could do was trust in time and hope it was something good. Rose didn't deserve anymore heartache in her life.

The train that Jimmy and Rose had been waiting for came to a stop just short of the buffers. Within a few minutes the passengers had left the train and the platform and the cleaning staff were busy about their business preparing for its next journey. Jimmy had about 15 minutes before the train was due to pull out. A chance to say his final goodbyes before setting off to his new adventure.

"I'm going to miss you Jimmy Deacon. You hurry and come home back to me."

"Hey, I'll be back before you know it. But please do me a favour and keep an eye on my mum and the kids while I'm gone. They've always had me with them to sort things out and I'm not sure how they're going to cope with me gone."

"Don't worry, I'll take good care of them. I've had a lot of practice with dad." It was the first time she could talk about her dad without filling up. Although it had only been a short time, she was coming to terms with the loss. Of course, it still hurt and she missed him terribly but she was beginning to let him go. Besides, she had a new purpose in her life now which was giving her renewed strength, not to mention the fact that she was now looking forward to taking care of a husband in the future. A thought that made her beam inside.

The time had come. The cleaning staff had signalled that the train was ready for boarding and the first of the passengers were stepping on to find their seats.

"Well this is it." Jimmy said as he stood. They kissed once last time, Jimmy picked up his small suitase and walked towards the train door. "Be good." he cheekily said with a smile. Rose smiled back and he stepped on to the train. He pulled the door shut behind him, pulled down the window and they stared at each other until the train started slowly moving. Within a few seconds the train was moving out of view at the end of the platform and Jimmy had gone. She turned away with a tear in her eye but still with a smile on her face. She would now count the days until he was back. (29,300)

CHAPTER FIFTEEN

FORBIDDEN...

Jimmy had been away at his basic training for three weeks and had been true to his word. He had written to Rose almost everyday telling her how he was progressing with his training. Every letter told her how much he couldn't wait to get home to marry her. That thought alone had kept him going through the early days of his training.

Jimmy's initial training was halfway through and he had been progressing well. He had been given the position of squad leader and already had the respect of his comrades. Most of the lads were aspiring aircrew candidates heading for radio operators, bomb crews or gunners but it would still be a few weeks before they each knew where they were headed. They all had the opportunity to put forward their own wish lists but aircrews were assigned to the squadrons that needed them most. In the current climate, aircrew positions were notoriously dangerous and few aircrews would survive their 30 mission tally without incident. Still, after 30 missions there would be a choice of becoming instructors. less dangerous positions or even a return to civvy street. Many would opt for a second active service posting rather than return to an easier life. For Jimmy, he was enjoying his new life and was eager to get past this basic stuff and get into a plane. Despite this, his heart still belonged to Church Street and Rosie.

Back on Church Street, life was almost as it was before the attack. The Swan was still closed but work was progressing well to return the old pub back to its glory days. It was the last area of the station that needed to be repaired but compared to the rest of the street the old structure was good. Rose's house had been completely demolished and there was now just a gap in the street where it once stood. Rose would walk past each morning on her way to work and look at where her life used to be with her dad. Everyday she would be tearful at the memories but by the time she had arrived at the station for work she was composed and busied herself with earning enough money to ensure she could pay her way at the Deacon's house.

Although things were just about back to normal on the station, the atmosphere was different. Of course, it was a lot quieter without Jimmy's voice bellowing out and the under-the-coat deals that he provided to the locals were sorely missed but there was something else. A sense of darkness filled the air as if the joy had been bombed out of the station. She couldn't quite put her finger on it but it was definitely different.

As for William, she had kept her distance. She would always say hello when she saw him but conversations were less and less. Regardless, she would watch him from a distance as he would repeat the same ritual each day. Still, everyday seemed to tale its toll on him and he appeared even weaker and more disconnected from his surroundings, as if he didn't care anymore where he was. Rose felt cautious about getting too close to him but couldn't help but feel a connection that made her feel sorry for him. She was confused in herself, of course she had a very real loving relationship with Jimmy but she also couldn't suppress her feelings for William. This was dangerous, any feelings for William couldn't be real, it seemed almost forbidden plus it could also destroy her relationship with Jimmy. May be the fact that a relationship seemed impossible was what was attracting her but she knew this was something she would need to keep in control.

William's torment continued. Everyday was more and more a struggle to just keep going, he He felt so weak that most of the day he would just stay sat on the bench by Platform 1 waiting for whenever he was needed.

He was aware of Rose watching him every now and then but he was also aware that she was keeping her distance from him. He hadn't felt so alone since he first arrived on the station. He wanted to talk to her, not for any specific reason, just because he liked her and talking to her gave him some comfort in this strange existence that he was in. He was missing her company and their talks but she hadnt been the same since Christmas which he thought was understandable. But even though she had explained that her outburst at him was just her venting, she still remained at a distance. He prayed that would change soon.

As evening rolled in on Church Street, the station had drawn almost to a complete stop. The last of the passengers had long left and the local businesses were closing up for the day. Rose had packed away her cart and was preparing to leave when she spotted William sat on his bench. A long time had passed since she had a proper conversation with him, something which she had been putting off mostly out of a guilty feeling after her outburst at him. Although the ice had been broken, she couldn't help feeling a distance between them which was her fault. The time had come to make the peace but she felt a sense of caution of not wanting to fall into the trap of getting too close. She walked over to him.

"Hello William, how are you feeling?" She could see just how terrible he looked now she was closer to him. His face had the appearance of parchment but grey in colour. His eyes were dark and heavy and he appeared to have lost all energy.

"Hello Rose" he answered with a slurred speech. "Honestly, I feel so tired. But I don't want to burden you with my problems, how are you holding up?"

"Oh, I'm OK, I'm just taking one day at a time. I've got plenty to keep my mind occupied and my hands busy so I'm thankful for that. Look, William, I've been wanting to talk to you properly about that day when... Well, you know. I just want you to know that I was just upset with everything that was happening and you were just in the firing line. I didn't mean to take it out on you, can you forgive me?"

"There's nothing to forgive, I understand how upset you were but I do need you to know something. I was there with you. I don't know what happened that day, all I know is nobody could see me and there was nothing I could do to warn anybody."

"It's OK, I know you were there. I don't know how I know but I feel it. I know you took some of my pain away William and I thank you for that. But I've got to be honest, I don't know what to think anymore, I guess that's why I've been avoiding you since that day. I know you don't mean anyone any harm and I know that what ever the reason for you being here, it's for good but it's so much to take in. I don't understand what's happening William and I'm pretty sure you don't either. I suppose time will tell us. She smiled and put her arms around him. "I'm sorry that I've not been around for you. I promise from now on, we'll have a chat everyday."

William felt the strength coming back into him. "It's OK Rose, you just make sure you take care of yourself, but there's no hard feelings. As long as we're OK now."

"We're OK." She got up ready to go home. "I suppose I better get back home. I've still got a lot to do this evening. I'll see you tomorrow William."

She turned and left him on the platfrom. As he watched her walk out of the station, he thought about how he was looking forward to seeing her again in the morning. It was the first thing he had looked forward to for a long time.

The following morning brought a whole new energy for William. He felt that he had somehow been recharged overnight and the tiredness that had pulled him down in recent weeks had gone. He couldn't help but wonder whether it was Rose, or at least her influence, that had renewed him. Was she the reason? Maybe his whole reason for being on the station had something to do with her. More questions for him to consider.

As usual, Rose arrived at the station and set up her cart ready for the day's trade. She busied herself setting up the fresh delivery of flowers into a beautiful arrangement into the manner that everybody had come to love. Her displays added a much needed beauty to the surroundings and somehow made a cold and functional building into a warm and friendly enviroment.

Today felt a little different. Her normal morning tears from being reminded of her dad as she passed where her house used to be, were absent. She felt happier than she had been since Christmas and it was a very welcome feeling. She had no idea why she felt this way, nor did she want to question it but she liked the feeling. Maybe she was just ready to move on from the awful events that had happened at the start of the year.

As she worked she looked across at where William usually sat, expecting to see the fading figure of the soldier she had come to know over the past few weeks. Instead, she saw William sat bolt upright, looking like he was posing for a military photograph. He too, looked different in a positive way, he looked strong again. She had to speak to him. She walked across to where he was sat.

"Good morning William, how are you today? You look different."

"Good morning Rose, I feel different. I don't feel as week as I have done. I don't know why, I just feel better. Better is good, right?"

"It's got to be. I've been very concerned about you just recently, it semed like you were fading away from us. But today, you seem... well, full of life." She paused at that last comment. Did he even have life in him, yes he looked better but he still didn't seem normal like everybody else.

"You know what I think?" he said. "I think it's something to do with you. When you stayed away from me, I felt week but as soon as you got close to me again, I felt stronger." Rose saw it too, he had got better since she started talking to him last night but surely it was just a coincidence. What power could she possibly have? She avoided going into the conversation any deeper. "It must be my pure magic." she joked. "Well, I better get back over to my cart and earn a few pennies, I'll talk to you a little later, William." William nodded at her with a smile and she turned and left.

The day passed in it's normal manner. William had the unfortunate job of comforting two families throughout the day. One was the family of a Spitfire pilot that had been killed in a training accident, the other, a soldier killed on the battlefield in Italy. As he expected both times took his energy from him leaving him feeling exhausted but he regained his strength quickly enough. He was sure the reason for this was Rose. As long as he stayed close to her he would be OK. But it wasn't just the fact that she gave him strength, he really liked her. He knew in himself that he couldn't get too close to her but the feelings of love were getting stronger and stronger and he was unsure whether he would be able to remain true to his morals. He knew very well that she was in love with Jimmy but Jimmy wasn't at home anymore to look after her. He had to be the one to do that, it was wrong to get too close but he would do anything to make sure she was safe and stayed happy. He just wished he could be with her once she left the station, he knew very little of her life away from Church Street, that's just the way it was.

As the station finally emptied of commuters and other coming and going passengers, the businesses were closing down for the evening once more. Rose was locking away her cart and preparing to leave just like she did every night. As she turned to leave, William was standing next to her, she jumped back, startled.

"Oh William, where did you come from? You made me jump."

"Sorry Rose, I didn't mean to scare you. I just thought I'd pop over and have a chat before you left."

"Oh, whats up?"

"Oh nothing really, I just wanted to make sure you were OK. I hope I didn't make you feel uncomfortable this morniing."

"Oh no," She replied. "I must admit, I don't know how little old me could be the reason you are better and I have to say, you do look so much better now." She was starting to drift as she looked at William. He did look out of place in the station but he was very handsome and she couldn't deny she felt a strong attraction towards him. She began thinking of what it would be like to be held by him in a loving way, maybe even kissing him... She snapped out of her train of thought realizing she was staring at him.

"Sorry, I was away with my thoughts there, What was I saying? Oh yes, You look so much stronger than you have been." She felt embarrassed and was now struggling to say something which hid the truth of her thoughts. Thankfully, William saved her.

"I do feel better but I'm still here doing exactly the same thing that brought me here before Christmas and I've still no answers to my questions. Is this my lot Rose? Is this where I will spend the rest of my time?"

Rose's previous embarrasment passed quickly as she now wanted to provide some kind of answer for her friend. He had asked it so many times before but she still couldn't be sure who or what William was. She moved a little closer to him and put her hand on his arm gently and tenderly.

"This will end for you William, I don't know how but I do know that a good soul like you would not be cursed by God. All I can think is you are here for a very good reason, you just can't see it yet but he is using you for a good reason. Maybe, for the time being, you should just let things be and see what happens. You're safe here and there are people that love you." She stopped talking as she realised what she had just said."

He was stunned but had to ask "Do you Rose, do you love me?"

She couldn't help herself, she leaned forward and kissed him. It was a long kiss and it felt wonderful and it felt... WRONG! She pulled away suddenly.

"I'm sorry William, I shouldn't have done that." She looked up to him and for a moment she saw him in a completely different way. The greying soldier she had come to know was suddenly gone to be replaced by a Handsome young man with a fresh complextion and Jet black hair staring back at her. His lips were smiling and full of colour and he had the most beautiful eyes she had ever seen. She was seeing William as he once was. She shook her head and looked again, William was as he was. What had just happened, she asked herself.

"No, I'm sorry Rose, I shouldn't have let that happen." He also felt guilty at the kiss. As wonderful as it was, he knew he would have to leave her at some point and besides, there was Jimmy. She loved Jimmy in ways that he could never be loved. But he didn't want to lose her again. "Let's just forget it. No damage done?"

"No damage done." She said. But she knew that kiss had affected her in so many ways. She could not tell Jimmy, that would kill him. Best just to try to pretend it didn't happen but she did have to speak honestly to William.

"Look William, you know I care for you very much and maybe if things were different... Well, you know. Besides, I've also got Jimmy to think about now and I can't break his heart."

"It's OK Rose. I know it can never be but I don't want you avoiding me anymore, I don't think I could handle that."

"I won't, I promise. We'll just look after each other until our next pages are turned."

Without saying another word, she pecked him on the cheek, smiled and left for home.

This night had left William thinking about his existence on the station once more. He was still capable of love despite what was happening to him. Was Rose right in what she was saying about being used for God? There were precious few alternative answers. But it still felt like a prison sentence, despite of all the good he was doing, and he did know the things he did were good, he was trapped on the station. He could walk out of the big entranceway and walk up Church Street a certain distance but whenever he walked too far he would suddenly find himself sat on the bench by Platform 1. There was no escape.

CHAPTER SIXTEEN

THE SKY'S THE LIMIT...

Jimmy's basic training was over, he had worked hard throughout the process and had come out as squad leader. He had taken to his new military life like a duck to water mastering everything that was thrown at him. Being the man of the house at home had groomed him for a life of responsibility and respect which made the discipline side of the RAF almost second nature. He was a natural hard worker and was never shy of coming forward and getting on with the tasks given to the recruits. In many cases, the other recruits looked to the confident cockney to help them overcome the hardships they encountered which did not go unnoticed by the hierarchy. He was given the position as squad leader and noted as future leadership material.

The conclusion of basic training allowed Jimmy to get back to Church Street for a few day to have a little time with his family and Rose before being shipped down to Devon for the next phase of his training. He was relieved to see that life was normal and nothing had happened since he had been away. The Luftwaffe had left the old street alone even though the attacks continued over the city. He was actually eager to get up in the air and stop the attackers from hurting anymore of his fellow Londoners, especially the ones he loved back on his Street and the Station. He enjoyed the time at home with Rose although he felt something was a little different. He couldn't quite put his finger on it but there was something. Maybe it was just the fact that he had been away for longer than he had every been away before and there was just a little awkwardness. He didn't worry too much about it as Rose's affections were still strong despite his feeling.

Before he knew it though, it was now back to training. He had volunteered for the position as a Tail End Charlie (Rear Gunner) in a Wellington Bomber and was now learning the skills needed to operate the four Browning .303 machine guns in very challenging situations.

He had to learn to strip and assemble the guns in under two minutes blindfolded to simulate maintenance in the dark. He would undergo live firing exercises on ranges in Wales simulating firing at moving planes. He would learn night vision skills and survival skills in the event of being shot down over land and water which included escape and evasion skills. The Wellington bomber was flown primarily on night operations at altitudes of up to 20,000ft for up to 10 hours at a time. The Tail Gunner was situated in a small turret at the rear with very little room to move around. The space was so cramped, the gunner could not wear his parachute while in the turret. In the case of an emergency, the tail-end charlie would have to pull himself out of the turret, retrieve his parachute and put it on before jumping out of the aircraft. The temperatures at flying altitude could reach as low as 40 degrees below so he would need to learn how to keep himself warm in the enclosed turret space. And of course there was also the sensation of flying in the rear of the aircraft which caused severe air sickness to the unaccustomed. These are all skills that Jimmy would have to learn and master over the next 12 weeks.

He found the first few weeks quite boring as it really just consisted of sitting around in classrooms listening to lectures that seemed to be more like a test of staying awake rather than learning subject matter. Most of what was being taught was common sense in his opinion and wasn't necessary information when being attacked by a Messerschmidt. He had already decided what was important, How to shoot and maintain the four .303 guns, knowing how to spot and shoot down the enemy and how to survive the many dangers he would face. However, he would need to know how to perform all of these tasks which lead to the many hours in lecture rooms learning about the aircraft he would meet, the guns he would shoot, etcetera.

Relief came firstly on the ranges learning to shoot at an improvised target from a turret mounted on an old truck. Of course, this would be nothing like the real thing but it did provide an opportunity to become accustomed to the recoil of the powerful weapon system and how to deal with problems such as stoppages and jams in a safe and steady environment. He loved the weapons training, especially the live firing. It gave him a big sense of exhilaration that he had never experienced before. It was a sense of power, power of life and death over anyone who dared to oppose him. But he also knew as the Tail Gunner, he was also responsible for the lives of his other crew mates and the aircraft when being attacked from the rear, something which he also found unnerving.

And then came his first flight. He was to go up in an Armstrong Whitworth Whitley, a twin engined mid range bomber used for training gunners by way of the mid and tail guns. Six cadets were assigned to each aircraft and would embark on various exercises from basic familiarisation to extreme corkscrew manoeuvres while operating the tailguns. Something which almost always lead to vomiting from the new recruits.

His first flight was pure exhilaration followed by a period of nausea which he fought hard to overcome all caused by the experienced pilots in the front throwing the aircraft around like a rag doll in the sky, much to their amusement. As funny as they found this, it was essential to prepare the new crews to the rigors of flight as soon as possible to ensure their future concentration was solely on their jobs. Once the aircraft had landed, each recruit would step off the aircraft pretending they felt fine and joking with feigned bravado hiding the fact that they felt very air sick but as soon as they were out of human sight, the truth made itself known in a violent and messy way.

Within a few weeks, Jimmy had become accustomed to the violent air movement combined with the smells of aviation fuel and cordite from the expelling guns and was becoming a very competent tail gunner. Many of the recruits had dropped out of the course and were know headed for other duties within the RAF such as ground crew, clerical duties or station defence. But Jimmy was doing well, he was thriving in the air which was being noticed by his aircrews and training officers. He would be someone they could rely on in times of crisis. As long as things remained on course, he would be a Sergeant at the end of his training which meant more money available to send home.

Live firing training at RAF Hell's Mouth in Wales had arrived and it was the most testing of the cadets training programme. They would fire upon targets dragged behind the aircraft with live ammunition in mock attacks over ranges purposely set aside for these exercises.

Jimmy had a good crew with him, he had become used to their flying style and trusted them to get the aircraft to where it was needed safely and quickly. However, this particular training exercise required an endurance phase where they would be airborne for three hours flying around the Welsh coast and over the sea simulating a cross channel mission. After three hours in the air they would return to the range to run a bombing training mission followed by a mock attack from the rear. Six aircraft in all would take part in the exercise and at the conclusion, those who successful achieved their mission would be presented with their brevets. In Jimmy's case, it would be the Air Gunners Wing.

Pre-flight preparations and briefing were now standard practice and passed without issue. Within and hour, Jimmy was once again strapping himself into the gun turret at the rear of the aircraft. Radios were tested and he then listened in as he heard the Pilot and Co-Pilot go through the drills of starting the engines. The airframe vibrated violently as the engines fired into life and the exhaust fumes leaked into the draughty turret.

"Tower, Whisky 6443 awaiting taxi instruction for departure to Hell's Mouth, over"

"Roger 6443, taxi straight to Runway 27 and hold short, over..."

And so the radio conversations continued giving directions, weather and wind information, instrument settings until the Whitley was sat on the threshold with its engines being run up to full power and the brakes being released. The noise increased dramatically and the plane shook violently as it rolled down runway 27 gaining speed quickly. From the tail turret the aircraft felt like it was shaking apart on take off, indeed, the sensations were at its worst here but Jimmy was becoming well used to it. The tail began to rise which told him the aircraft was approaching take-off speed, a few seconds later the vibrations eased as the plane gently left the ground. Almost instantly, the tail yawed off making a crabbing sensation which the Pilot quickly corrected with gentle rudder inputs. Once again, they were flying.

Jimmy had a good hour before he was needed apart from the occasional radio check which he was positive was just the Pilot making sure he hadn't dropped off to sleep. He stared out of the turret glass at Wales below, it was something he felt he could never get used to, in a good way. The view was breathtaking. He felt lucky that only a few would experience what he was seeing, those tail-end-charlies who would look out on to what had passed in all its magnificence. He reached inside his jacket and pulled out his writing pad and pen and did his best to share with Rose his experience as it was happening. He began with how he missed and loved her, he asked after his family and all of those at the station and then started telling of her how he was sat in the clouds looking down over everything. He told her of how beautiful and small the world looked from where he sat and felt like he was some kind of angel overseeing the wonders of God. In this moment, he had never felt more alive...

"Hello Whisky Tango 5, this is Whisky Tango (WT) 1, radio check over." WT5 was Jimmy's callsign within the aircraft.

"Roger WT1, this is WT5, all clear over."

Roger WT5, we are approaching the coast, keep your eyes out for bandits over."

This was the signal for the first part of the exercise. An air attack would be simulated by the on-board instructor calling "Fighter Coming In On Port — Stand By! — Corkscrew Port — Go!"

Those were the words that all bomber crews hated to hear, the odds were not in their favour. Their aircraft were slower than the fighter, less manoeuvrable, and heavily laden with 1,000s of gallons of petrol, oil and of course the bomb load. Any of which, could easily ignite or explode from a single cannon shell being placed in just the right location. The bombers defences were limited offensively; and while "Kills" were claimed by Bomber Crew Gunners, it was more luck than a gunner would have the time and more importantly the range of his guns to be able to fend off a fighter, let alone inflict sufficient damage upon it to force it to break off or better still to be shot down. However, the combination of the gunners reactions and the "Corkscrew" manoeuvre was often was enough to give the bomber and its crew a fighting chance or at least cause the fighter to miss its target and maybe break off to find another prey. Therefore the theory behind preventing an attack was to "prevent being detected", or if detected "finish the combat without being seriously damaged.

Thus the Corkscrew Manoeuvre or Barrel Roll was developed. Designed to present the bomber to the fighter in a manner that the fighter could line up for attack and at the moment the attack began, the direction and altitude of the bomber would be violently changed through a series of direction and altitude changes.

From flying straight and level, the Snap Order came from the crew, "Corkscrew Port" or "Starboard, Go!". Immediately the plane went right over until the wings were almost vertical, and at the same time, straight down as hard as possible. When the airspeed reached somewhere around 350 or 400 knots, the aircraft rolled off the other way, and then climbed as steep as it could until it was almost stalling, and then round, and down again, flying through the sky on a Corkscrew or Helical path.

It wasn't long before the order came through. In next to no time the plane was going through it violent course of going up and down and side to side until the order 'Tail Clear' came through simulating the end of the attack. Jimmy hardly had anytime to think, from the start to its finish but his actions had become automatic as he found himself swinging the turret through its arcs tracking the imaginary aircraft.

From that moment on it was all go. Preparations for the bombing run were now in motion. For Jimmy, all he could do was sit, observe and wait until the bomb run had finished before he would be needed once more when he would be needed to shoot down the simulated target which would be dragged behind.

Over the next 30 minutes the aircraft went through its dance of approaching the target, releasing live ordanance and then climbing back out to rejoin the pack. Each plane took its turn until all had run the gauntlet. It was then back out to seas, turn around and then back to the ranges to simulate the aerial attack. One of the most vulnerable times for a bomber was on its way back home after the attack. The crew had already spent hours in the air, the aircrafts fuel was depleting and the airframe may have received damage from anti-aircraft artillery (Ack-Ack). Those were most at danger as they would be limping back home damaged and presenting themselves as easy targets. Like an African predator, the Luftwaffe would seek out the sick and wounded as easy prey so the crew would need to be at its most alert during these times. It was easy to become complacent as they approached home so extra concentration and vigilance was needed.

The exercise would be aimed at Jimmy's turret when the training target would be released to trail behind. Again the 'Corkscrew' order would be voiced over the radio and the plane would begin its drill throwing Jimmy's senses into array. The action would make the towed target act erratically making it almost impossible to hit. Jimmy fought with his senses concentrating hard to focus on the target while looking for friendly aircraft while traversing the turret. Within seconds he brought the four brownings on to the ideal trajectory and pressed the trigger and fired a burst. Almost instantly, the target shredded and separated from the towing line. Jimmy had scored a direct hit. He signaled his victory in a calm an official-like manor over the radio.

"WT1, this is WT5, enemy aircraft destroyed, tail clear, over."

"WT5, Roger, Tail Clear." the Captain repeated. He then added. "Bloody good shooting Jimmy, well done."

Jimmy sat back in his seat feeling relieved and very pleased with himself. All that was left was to relax and enjoy the ride home. Before that though, the final two aircraft would repeat the exercise that Jimmy had just completed. Jimmy's aircraft would stay in formation to simulate the reality of an attack on each aircraft while heading home giving the pilot the opportunity to hone his skills in avoiding friendly aircraft. The plane being attacked would drop back allowing the other trainers to keep out of the line of fire and to keep out of the way of the spiraling airframe.

For Jimmy, he had a ringside seat to watch the fun. He watched the dragging target released and then the plane went into its Corkscrew drill. As the aircraft dived, he lost view of it for a few moments. When it re-appeared it had gained on the pack and had leveled off close to his plane. Jimmy got straight on the radio.

"WT1, this is WT5, you might want to warn WR that he is very close to our aircraft. Advise he drops back, over."

WT5, Roger."

He watched the Whitley sink once more. The Captain had

warned him and was taking avoiding action. He kept his eye on the area he last saw the aircraft. For what seemed like an age there was nothing. It seemed like the skipper had got his message across and WR had got out of the danger zone. Then all of a sudden, it appeared directly below Jimmy and was rising to meet him. There was nothing he could do.

He saw Rose as he closed his eyes and felt her kiss on his lips. He saw his mum and the kids as they were at Christmas time enjoying themselves as they played. and then...

WR had increased its speed too much on the dive and had come up right under Jimmy's plane. As they collided, WR lurched to the left and the two starboard wings smashed into each other igniting instantly. The ensuing explosion destroyed both aircraft leaving only debris and the remainder of the two burning fuselages to fall uncontrollably to earth. Nobody survived.

CHAPTER SEVENTEEN

QUESTIONS ANSWERED...

The train was due in at 6:00pm. It was the last train of the day and it was the one Rose had been waiting for. Jimmy had been away for 12 weeks and according to his letters he had been doing really well. He had completed his final flight yesterday and she was looking forward to seeing him in his uniform wearing his wing patch. The whole station would be proud of him but they could see him tomorrow. She hadn't told anyone he was coming home, tonight he was hers.

Her excitement had been overwhelming all day long for her. She had been quietly planning their wedding while he was away, there was no date yet, just plans on how they would do it. If she could get things organised then it would give them both something to look forward to.

She had noticed William had not been on the station today. Perhaps he was keeping a low profile following their moment some weeks ago. Things had been friendly since but cautious on both parts. They had come close to crossing the line and they could not let it happen again. She knew how William felt for her and thought that her reunion with Jimmy may have been a little awkward and painful for him. She didn't feel anything was wrong so it was natural to assume her thoughts were justified.

In truth, William had been with her all day long. He had felt Jimmy's final moments and knew what was coming but like before, he was now unseen to her yet again. This time, he understood. He would need to be with her as she learnt the news of his death. She was going to be crushed and he wasn't sure he could do anything to help her.

He sat on his bench by platform 1 watching Rose and waiting for the inbound train. There was still half an hour before it was due, each minute seeming like a lifetime, ticking away like some slowed down clock drawing out the pain further and further until the moment he dreaded would arrive.

As he sat waiting, a soldier approached William and sat on the bench next to him. At first he ignored his presence but something made him take notice. The soldier was dressed in the same uniform as him and was very familiar. Then it hit him, it was Captain John Rogers, his old Platoon Commander from France. William was beyond shocked, he didn't believe what was happening.

"What's going on?" William asked the Officer.

"Hello William, nice to see you again."

"Again, what the hell is going on? Am I imagining this?"

"No William, you're not. I'm real, or as real as you are. You've done a great job here but it's time to go, I've come to take you home."

"Home?" William was confused. "What home? I've been here for months and I don't know any home. Do you know why I've been here?"

Captain Rogers smiled. "You've known all along why you were here, you just didn't want to admit it to yourself. You've been like a guardian angel watching over your friend there," He pointed to Rose. "She has needed one since Christmas but after tonight she will be OK. She needed you to guide her through everything that has happened to her and you've done a wonderful job. You've helped so many people and not once thought about helping yourself. You should be very proud. But it's now time to move on. Everyone is waiting for you."

William, looked broken as his new companion spoke for he knew his time here was coming to an end.

"I can't go yet," he said. "I have to stay with Rose until she learns of Jimmy."

"Don't worry, Jimmy is going to say goodbye to her himself. He'll be with her when the train arrives. She's going to be just fine."

"Still, I want to wait. I need to make sure for myself."

"Ok, It's your choice. But I'll be waiting over here."

William nodded just as the whistle of the approaching train sounded. He moved on to the Platform towards Rose who was already waiting. He waited alongside her.

The train quickly emptied and in a few minutes she was standing alone on Platform 1. She was alone and knew something had happened. Tears started streaming down her face as she thought, not Jimmy, not my wonderful Jimmy. She was motionless, she knew in that moment he wasn't coming home. She had no idea of what had happened, there had been no news and nobody had told her or his family, but she knew. And then she felt Williams hand on her shoulder. She couldn't see him but she knew he was there.

"William?" she sobbed "Are you here?" she turned and William was standing next to her.

"I am Rose, I'm so sorry." He was doing his best to take her pain but he couldn't feel anything inside.

"What happened, do you know?" She asked. She seemed almost calm and composed despite her tears.

"I'm sorry, I don't. All I know is it happened yesterday. I wish I could take his place and give him back to you."

"I loved him, I loved him so much William."

"I know you did" the words didn't come from William. She looked past him and standing behind was an airman in full flying gear smiling at her.

"I love you too, Rose." It was Jimmy standing before her. William moved away and watched as they came together.

"Jimmy, is it really you? I thought you was..."

"I am, Rose." He cut her off. "I just needed to be sure that you were going to be OK and you will be. You are going to grow old and happy, and you'll have a great life."

She hugged him, he felt cold.

"Please don't go Jimmy, please don't leave me."

"I have to, my darling. I need you to be brave for me, just one more time. You need to be the one to take care of all of these people now. My family are going to need you more than ever, as well as everyone on the old station. We will be watching over you, always. I can promise you that."

"We?" Rose asked.

"It's time for William to go too. He's been here all of this time to look after you and everyone in the station until this moment.

He's finished now and must move on with me. It's his time to go now."

She looked across at William and smiled at him. Despite her sadness she felt happy that William was finally moving on. She would miss him too. He looked back at her with sadness in his eyes. Her sadness. He was helping her one last time.

Jimmy hugged Rose once more and then broke contact with her.

"I'll always love you and I'll always be with you in your heart. I'll be there when you need me."

"I love you so much Jimmy."

Jimmy walked over to William and Captain Rogers and stood beside them. All of a sudden Rose ran over to Jimmy and William and hugged them both, one in each arm. And then they were gone.

Rose looked at the spot where they had been standing just a few moments before, and stared at the empty space. They were both gone now, and that was that, In the space of no more than half an hour, she had lost the love of her life and said goodbye to the mysterious soldier who had haunted Church Street station since before Christmas. Before the 'half hour', life was good. She was looking forwards to becoming Mrs Rose Deacon and looking forwards to the end of the war when they would settle down and spend the rest of their lives together. But despite her sense of loss and deep sadness, she knew Jimmy, William and her dad were all OK. Finally she knew it. They were at peace, in a place where there was no war, no pain, no sadness. She would see them again, she was sure of that but she had a long life to live first, and to begin with she needed to go home to the Deacon house and be there for his mother and the kids.

His mum was going to be so hurt, of course losing her son was going to be devastating. He had been her strength ever since the death of her husband, Jimmy's father. But it was more than that, she relied on Jimmy in so many ways. He had been the man of the house and the bread winner for many years and now it was going to be Rose's job. She needed to be the strength. Maybe everything that had happened over the past few months had lead Rose to this destiny. Maybe she was meant to do this all along. Maybe William had kept her safe so she would understand, at this moment, what destiny was going to ask of her. She had a new family that she needed to look after from now on.

She would mourn the passing of Jimmy and she would miss him so much in her life, but she would have mum and the kids to help her through it and she would do the same for them. They would be strong together, they would cry together and then they would eventually laugh together. They would now become a family together,

She looked at the bench by Platform 1 and pictured the mysterious soldier sitting there. His time was finally over. Was he an angel looking over the station or was he just a lost spirit looking for his eternal peace? He had helped so many people in the short time he had spent at the station, so many lost souls were comforted. Was that his task, or did he just play it out because that was the man he was in his former life? She was finished asking questions about him. Whoever and whatever he was it was no longer important. She would just remember him as the Spirit of Christmas 1940.

She turned and walked out of Church Street station, knowing that tonight was going to be a long night....

EPILOGUE

Church Street Station, Christmas Eve 1999 and Mrs Rose Kingsley had come back to the old building one more time just as she had done every year since the end of World War 2. Once the war had finished she moved out of the station and found a small shop in the city where she would establish her business, 'Deacon's Flowers'. As the years rolled on by the small shop grew until a chain of stores brought her success and eventually a husband. She had met Tom Kingsley when he had come in to buy flowers to put on the grave of his father, a Bomber pilot who was killed in a training accident over Wales during the war. Their obvious history became the cornerstone for their life together.

Tom would become a wonderful husband, a loving stepfather and eventually a proud father to two boys, James and William. They were all here on Christmas Eve to help the ageing Rose and Tom visit for the final time. The old station was a mass of electronic billboards, hi-tech shops, a rush of faceless commuters and the very latest technology ensuring the bustling metropolis ran smoothly.

The old bench remained by platform 1, but was seldom used. Folks these days just didn't have the time to sit and read a paper or chat to other station users. But Rose wondered if William's Spirit visited from time to time. Of course, the war was now a long time in the past, and it was no longer a place of such immense sadness, but maybe the people who travelled through the turnstiles would benefit from his touch every now and then.

As for the rest of the station, a popular coffee chain now served where Sally once shouted over cups of tea, and The Swan was now an upmarket wine bar. Rose looked around, times had changed, people had moved on, but the Station remained.

Before she left the station for the final time she handed a plaque to the station manager, John Crispin; to be placed on the bench by Platform 1. It read 'To live in the hearts we leave behind, is not to die'....

Printed in Great Britain
by Amazon

11677368R00071